"In case you have failed to observe it, I am not a boy. I am a man. I am not attracted to girls, but to women—like you." As he spoke, he put one arm around her waist and pulled her against him. His head came down, and before she knew what he was about, his hot lips had seized hers in a scorching kiss.

Her immediate reaction was outrage, tinged with disbelief. This couldn't be happening! But it was—that rock-hard chest, those strong arms, were all too real. She struggled, then before the embrace degenerated into a wrestling match, he released her. Without thinking of the consequences, she raised her hand and slapped his cheek with all the force she could muster. . . .

By Joan Smith
Published by Fawcett Books:

THE SAVAGE LORD GRIFFIN
GATHER YE ROSEBUDS
AUTUMN LOVES: An Anthology
THE GREAT CHRISTMAS BALL
NO PLACE FOR A LADY
NEVER LET ME GO
REGENCY MASQUERADE
THE KISSING BOUGH
A REGENCY CHRISTMAS: An Anthology
DAMSEL IN DISTRESS
A KISS IN THE DARK
THE VIRGIN AND THE UNICORN
A TALL DARK STRANGER
TEA AND SCANDAL
A CHRISTMAS GAMBOL
AN INFAMOUS PROPOSAL
PETTICOAT REBELLION

PETTICOAT REBELLION

Joan Smith

FAWCETT CREST • NEW YORK

A Fawcett Crest Book
Published by Ballantine Books
Copyright © 1997 by Joan Smith

All rights reserved under International and Pan-American Copyright Conventions. Published in the United States by Ballantine Books, a division of Random House, Inc., New York, and simultaneously in Canada by Random House of Canada Limited, Toronto.

http://www.randomhouse.com

Library of Congress Catalog Card Number: 96-97171

ISBN 0-449-22553-4

Manufactured in the United States of America

First Edition: April 1997

10 9 8 7 6 5 4 3 2 1

Chapter One

When Miss Slatkin summoned one of her school-mistresses to her office, the victim went trembling. Now, as Abbie Fairchild walked down the dim corridor to answer such a summons, she ransacked her mind, trying to discover how she might have displeased her employer. There had been an altercation regarding the quantity of paper used, but Slats, as her charges called Miss Slatkin behind her back, had already reprimanded her for that. Abbie was only a day mistress, teaching art to the young ladies at the academy five days a week. She consoled herself that if she were to be turned off, at least she had a home to go to.

Each morning at a quarter to nine, she left home and was accompanied the three blocks to the academy through the dangerous thoroughfares of residential Maidstone by a footman. At four o'clock, he was waiting to accompany her home. The income from her work, while negligible, gave her a modicum of independence. Of equal importance, it allowed her to escape for a few hours the stifling atmosphere of her uncle's house.

Colonel Fairchild's heart was in the right place, but his interests occupied an extremely narrow channel. And his interest was the battle of Mysore.

He knew it intimately, the way a clock maker knows the workings of a watch. Abbie had relived that battle on the undulating Deccan plateau in southern India with her uncle so many times that she knew all the ins and outs of it. Countless times she'd been told how, while the English had been losing the American colonies, Warren Hastings—and Colonel Fairchild, of course—had kept the Indian empire intact for the crown. She was familiar with the limitations of the Treaty of Mangalore, which had eventually terminated the battle. And she knew as much about the cause of the strife, the wily Hyder Ali, as she knew about her hero, Leonardo da Vinci—in fact, a good deal more.

Half an hour after she entered Miss Slatkin's lair, she emerged with an expression caught between a frown and a thrill of anticipation. The frown was due to her uncle's habitual reluctance to part with her; the thrill was the prospect of a week at Penfel Hall. It would be a week in paradise! She had toured the great house three times with her uncle. Her particular goal on the first visit had been the fabulous art gallery that held, among its myriad treasures, a painting of a fifteenth-century lady reputed to be an early da Vinci. It was on that visit that a chance remark of the guide told her of the da Vinci cartoons, which were, unfortunately, not on view to the public. These were preliminary sketches in pastel or charcoal on paper, some of which had eventually resulted in paintings, some of which had gone no further than the sketch.

She had written to Lord Penfel, asking for permission to view the cartoons. A month later his secretary, Mr. Singleton, had answered that his lordship regretted he could not oblige her, because the cartoons were too fragile to be handled by the public. A second request, written on stationery from Miss Slatkin's Academy and signed "Miss Abigail Fairchild, Art Teacher," had been answered more promptly, but no more helpfully. His lordship was not at home, but the policy at Penfel Hall was that only serious artists were invited to view the fragile artworks. Although Mr. Singleton did not say so, she read between the lines that only gentlemen were serious artists. She would have claimed to be Thomas Lawrence if she were a man. As she was only a lady, she had regretfully given up applying, but she had not given up hoping.

And now her hopes were answered. She was to be at Penfel Hall for a week as a guest, and she would finally see those treasures—even if she had to steal the key and knock a guard on the head with a poker to achieve it.

Her uncle seldom surprised her, but on that fateful afternoon, he absolutely astonished her.

"Excellent!" he cried, when she told him. "A week at Penfel Hall, you will enjoy that, Abbie. And it will just suit me. Major Thomas, my old army friend from India—we fought at Mysore together—has invited me to visit him in London." He gave her a warm smile and said foolishly, "You would be bored in London." Bored! How often had she urged him? But the thirty-five-mile trip in a well-sprung carriage only to see the great masterpieces of painting at Somerset House and the British Museum was not to be thought of. Nothing less than a resurrection of Mysore could accomplish it.

"It seems old Thomas is writing a book about the Mysore campaign and wants me to give him a hand," the colonel continued. "Thomas was not on the front line. There are a good many stories I can tell him. Oh, my, yes. I will never forget when Hyder Ali

3

landed the first rocket in on us. It was like fire falling from heaven. I remember . . ."

While Colonel Fairchild remembered his glory days, Abbie nodded and smiled and said "Oh, my!" in all the correct places, and thought her own thoughts. Miss Slatkin had explained that the visit was due to the annual spring holiday, when most of the girls would be returning home for a week. Lady Susan Anthrop's family, however, were not at their ducal home, Wycliffe. They were visiting Dugal Castle, one of their other estates in Scotland. Miss Slatkin had naturally offered to allow Lady Susan to remain at the academy, but the duchess had other ideas. Her cousin, the dowager Lady Penfel, had invited Lady Susan along with "a few friends" to stay with her at nearby Penfel Hall. Of course, one of their mistresses must accompany the young ladies. Miss Slatkin immediately chose Miss Fairchild as the most socially acceptable of her mistresses, and the likeliest to have suitable clothes.

"Her Grace perhaps hopes to forward a match between Lady Susan and Lord Penfel, but her timing is off," Miss Slatkin confided. "I read in the social column that Lord Penfel is on the verge of offering for Lord Peevey's daughter. He is visiting her at Lewes. Just as well," she added, with a knowing nod. "I would dislike to see three of my girls pitched into that gentleman's house if he were in residence. Quite a way with the ladies, one hears, and his mama, you know, is a widgeon. One could not count on Lady Penfel to keep him under control, and he is so handsome I make no doubt Kate and Annabelle would fall under his spell."

Miss Slatkin kept close track of all the noble bachelors. It was a point of pride when one of her graduates landed a title, but it was not such rascals as the dashing Lord Penfel with whom she wished her ladies to be associated. Abigail had never seen Lord Penfel, though she had heard rumors of him from the older girls. She was happy to learn he would not be at the Hall to make access to the cartoons difficult.

Lady Susan had chosen Kate Fenshaw and Annabelle Kirby to accompany her. Kate was a lively girl who had made herself a great favorite with all the students. Annabelle's papa was a wealthy brewer, second only to Samuel Whitbread in importance. As Whitbread was to porter, so Kirby was to light ale.

Lady Susan had five brothers. She often told Annabelle how much she would like the youngest, Lord Sylvester. It was generally assumed that Lord Sylvester would also like Annabelle's fat dowry. Even a duke must hustle to see five sons profitably settled.

"What arrangements have been made for the trip, Abbie?" her uncle asked.

"We will be leaving in Miss Slatkin's carriage on Monday morning. Penfel Hall is only twenty-five miles away. We shall be there for lunch. Miss Spadger will be following on the public coach to help take care of the girls' toilettes and so on. I shall chaperon them for outings, with Lady Penfel in charge. As Penfel Hall has such a famous collection, Miss Slatkin suggested I might give them some instruction on art appreciation while we are there."

"It will be a nice little holiday for you." He reached for his well-thumbed diaries. "Meanwhile, I shall be giving old Tom a hand with his book. I have just been looking up my notes on Mysore. Tom would know nothing of the Treaty of Mangalore. He was only a lieutenant in those days. I see here I have the temperatures recorded. Eighty-nine degrees. Imagine

5

fighting in such a cauldron as that! The perspiration was dripping down our faces and backs as if we were in a Turkish bath."

Abbie mentally packed her trunk while he thumbed through his diaries, mentioning hellish temperatures, abominable food, illness, and the constant racket of gunfire and rockets.

The weekend was busy preparing for her uncle's trip and her own. There was the laundering and packing to see to, along with the usual last-minute purchases of stockings, ribbons, and gloves. One did not visit Penfel Hall in soiled gloves. As well as her clothing, her art supplies had to be assembled. Her aim was not only to study the da Vinci cartoons but also to make copies of them. Only by attempting to copy did one learn the tricks of the masters. There was also a Chardin painting, *Girl with Rose*, she hoped to copy, if time allowed. Chardin portrayed a girl of perhaps twelve years sitting in profile, holding a rose. It was Abbie's hope to become a famous portrait painter. Being a lady and living in a small town in Kent made the necessary contacts difficult, but if she could get a commission from Lady Penfel, she would be on her way to becoming a serious artist.

Chapter Two

Her uncle's carriage left home at eight o'clock in the morning. The discipline of rising early, practiced during his many years in the army, had stayed with him in his retirement. At nine o'clock, Miss Slatkin's plain black traveling carriage with three trunks strapped on top drew up to Abbie's front door. The coachman and one footman had difficulty finding a spot for Miss Fairchild's trunk, but eventually got it stowed in the basket at the rear. Miss Slatkin, a famous skint, had not put herself to the expense of hiring four horses for the trip, and she had made it plain to the coachman that he was to keep to a sedate pace so there would be no need to stop to change nags along the way.

The trip of twenty-five miles took three hours. It was spring. Fortunately, the weather was fine and the scenery beautiful. The green meadows were dappled gold with cowslips. Sleek brown cows, placid as statues, grazed in pastures, and sheep dotted the hillsides like gray boulders. As April ended, the orchards of Kent were coming into full blossom. It was enough to make Abbie wish she could paint scenery. The orchards flaunted their frothy white petals, delicately tinted with pink. Birds rioted in the branches, filling the air with birdsong.

"Isn't it beautiful!" Kate Fenshaw cried, leaning her head out the window. She had removed her bonnet to allow her black curls to wanton in the wind. Her dark eyes glowed with health and youth. "It looks as if the trees were hung with cotton batting."

"It has been a late spring, and so the harvest will be late this year," Lady Susan informed them. Her elegant bonnet had not left her head, nor would it until she was inside Penfel Hall. Beneath the small brim, her haughty face wore its habitual expression of dutiful daughter, which consisted of resignation tinged with ennui. Her eyes were a pale blue; her hair blond, her features regular.

"At Wycliffe we have one hundred and fifty acres in apples," she announced. "I trust Beaton has had the smudge pots out to keep the buds from being nipped with frost at night."

"I hate apples," said Kate, whose papa also had a large orchard. His wealth, however, accrued from his coal mine. She yawned into her fist, then brightened when she observed an inn some distance ahead. "Could we stop for some tea, Miss Fairchild?" she asked. "I am starving."

Lady Susan gave a damping frown. "Certainly not! Ladies are never starving. You may feel peckish, but never hungry. Young ladies in an inn unaccompanied! It would be improper."

"We are not unaccompanied. We have Miss Fairchild."

"Ladies do not enter a public inn without a gentleman's escort."

"Perhaps the coachman could come with us, or the footman," Annabelle suggested.

"They are not gentlemen, Belle," Lady Susan explained.

"Miss Slatkin said we should not stop en route," Abbie said, "but she has packed a bottle of lemonade, if you are thirsty, Miss Fenshaw."

Four small glasses of weak lemonade were poured and consumed.

A few miles later, Kate stretched out her legs and wiggled her toes. "My bottom is falling asleep. I want to get out and move. I shall ask John Groom to stop and let me walk beside the carriage. I wager he is not moving above two or three miles an hour."

"We have gone sixteen miles in two hours," said Lady Susan, consulting her map. "We are going eight miles an hour."

"We'll never get there!" Kate complained.

"We shall be there in slightly over one hour, barring accidents," Lady Susan informed her.

"Why don't we sing, or play a game to pass the time?" Annabelle suggested.

"Let us recite our lessons," Lady Susan said. Kate groaned. "We shall recite the kings and queens of England, beginning with the Norman invasion. In 1066, King William I, died 1087. From 1087 to 1100, William II. Then 1100, Henry I, died 1135. You continue, Kate."

"In 1135, Henry II," Kate said.

"No, no! You are forgetting King Stephen, the nephew of Henry I. From 1135 to 1154. It was Stephen who adopted Arabic numerals."

"I hate Arabic numerals," Kate said.

"No, you hate Roman numerals," Lady Susan told her.

"Them, too. Why do they have to use letters?"

"I always prefer English numbers myself," Annabelle said.

Lady Susan, with a thought to her brother Sylvester, only smiled her dismay, then said to Kate,

9

"I don't know why you have so much difficulty with Roman numerals. It is really very simple." She was soon diverted from the kings of England to explaining how the Roman numerical system worked.

By the time they reached Penfel Hall, they had finished the lemonade and enjoyed, or at least endured, a lecture on Roman numerals, the value of learning Latin and Greek, and a diatribe on the desecration of Roman antiquities, along with a description of a Roman museum her papa, the duke, was setting up at Wycliffe. "Lord Sylvester is overseeing it," she said to Annabelle. "He is vastly interested in Roman antiquities, you must know."

"I didn't know he was in Rome," Annabelle said. She had about as much interest in Roman antiquities as she had in algebra, but considerable interest in Lord Sylvester, as she had never seen this noble stripling. She listened in confusion as Lady Susan explained that there were Roman antiquities aplenty in England, especially at Wycliffe, and refrained from inquiring how they had got there, for Lady Susan was sometimes quite sharp with her when she asked the wrong questions.

After a longish drive, Kate jumped in her seat. "There is Penfel, at last!" she cried, pointing to the left. "Isn't it beautiful?"

"Quite like a miniature Elmgrove," Lady Susan said, with a condescending glance at the Hall and just a slight emphasis on the "miniature." "James Gibbs, the same architect who restored our left wing, built Penfel in the seventeen hundreds. He was greatly influenced by Kent, of course."

"Kent is very pretty," Annabelle said.

"I am referring to William Kent, the architect,

10

landscape artist, and furniture designer, Belle. He was very good, although he was from Yorkshire. The style is pure Palladian."

She continued to give a résumé of the characteristics of the Palladian style. No one listened. Kate and Annabelle could have cared less. Abbie was quite as familiar as Lady Susan with the characteristics of Palladio, and could see for herself the classical symmetry of the house, the columned front, the pediment and cupola, the curving colonnades that finished in a large, sweeping wing on either side. The stone had weathered to the golden warmth of honey.

"Kent's park was reworked by Capability Brown," Lady Susan continued. "The winding water you see is dammed by a ruled dyke. There are extensive views in all directions. The eighteenth century insisted on an unbounded view."

Annabelle frowned. She could see very well that the view was bounded by the horizon, but she did not risk Lady Susan's wrath by mentioning it.

The carriage drew up in front of the pedimented doorway, and the ladies were assisted from the carriage by the one footman Miss Slatkin had provided to accompany her charges. The great oaken door was thrown open, and they were duly admitted into a square central hall that rose two stories, terminating in a ceiling window that allowed sunlight to fall on the marble floor below, and the marble statues set into niches. A series of doors around the square gave glimpses of the stately rooms beyond. Each doorway had a pilaster and pediment; some featured marble figures as large as life, reclining on the sides of the pediments. They appeared to represent culture. One held a book, one a flute, another a lute, one a globe, and one an astrolabe.

11

All this finery was brought to earth by a gentleman's curled beaver tossed rakishly on the head of a Roman statue of an athlete, with a chiffon scarf tied around its ankle.

"Good day, Sifton," Lady Susan said to the butler. She had visited the Hall five years before, and never forgot a name or a face connected in any way with the nobility.

"Your ladyship," he replied, bending at the waist.

Sifton led them to a door that would have allowed a haywain to pass without disturbing its cargo, and announced, "Lady Susan and her guests, your ladyship."

The room was so overwhelming, with molded cornices, two marble fireplaces, splendid portraits in gilded frames, masses of flowers, bronze busts on tables, and a great deal of heavy, carved furnishings, that one was inclined to overlook the déclassé-looking dame on the sofa. The most remarkable thing about Lady Penfel, in Abbie's view, was that she resembled an aging light-skirt. She wore her hair *à la mouton*. The frizz of tight curls about her hagged, rouged face was an unlikely bronze hue. Her stylish crepe gown was that hard-to-wear shade of blue called ultramarine, that looked best on ruddy-faced sailors.

Lady Susan strode forward and placed a kiss on the lined cheek. She introduced Miss Fairchild and her school friends.

After a few words of greeting and inquiry for various members of Susan's family, Lady Penfel said, "Don't let me detain you, ladies. I'm sure Miss Fairfield has plans for you. Sifton will show you to your rooms and give you anything you need. Hot water, a nice cup of tea . . ."

Her voice trailed off as she lifted the copy of *The Ladies Magazine* she held on her lap and stuck her nose into it. Lady Susan led the group away.

"What a quiz!" Kate said, stifling a snicker.

"Her ladyship must be feeling poorly," Lady Susan explained. "No doubt that is why she mispronounced your name, Miss Fairchild."

"That's odd," Annabelle said. "My Aunt Esther has been dying forever, and she remembers everything."

"Your Aunt Esther, if I recall, is not a countess," Susan replied.

"No, she has no head for numbers at all."

Kate poked Abbie in the ribs. "I wonder how a duchess behaves when she is poorly," she said in a low tone. "She probably forgets her own name. I noticed Lady Penfel didn't forget to use her rouge pot."

"Personal remarks are never in good taste, Miss Fenwick," Abbie replied as severely as she could, then spoiled the lesson by smiling.

"Aren't we going to have any luncheon?" Annabelle asked. "I am so hung—Oh, sorry, Lady Susan. I am feeling so peckish, I could eat a cow."

Abbie did not chastise her. She was hungry herself. What a strange visit it was going to be. But of one thing she felt confident. Without Lord Penfel to forbid it, she could easily convince that silly lady to show her the da Vinci cartoons.

Chapter Three

Sifton had the guests shown to the west wing, where they occupied four stately chambers, two on one side of the corridor, two across from them. Lady Susan's and Annabelle's rooms looked out on the front of the estate, Abbie's and Kate's on the rear. Abbie was gratified to see she was being treated as a real lady—a guest, rather than a sort of higher class of servant. Her room was charming, with dainty French furnishings and green damask hangings. The paintings in a room were always of particular interest to her, and she noticed that the Penfel love of art was not confined to the gallery. Her room held exquisite Flemish flower paintings. She would have preferred pictures of people, but she knew enough about art to appreciate what she saw.

She strolled to one of a pair of tall windows and gazed out, hugging to herself how fortunate she was to be here. All views were unbounded, as befit an estate designed in the eighteenth century. Abbie's view was of the walled home garden below, with es-paliered fruit trees forming intricate designs against the golden stone. Neat rows of vegetables extended the length of the enclosure. Two gardeners worked over the rows.

Beyond the walls was a meadow, with a forest

forming a backdrop in the distance. Abbie wondered at the unwonted activity going forth in the meadow. It looked as if tents were being erected. Surely gypsies were not setting up camp this close to Penfel! With the three young ladies on the estate, this seemed dangerous. Yet she disliked to tell Lady Penfel her duty. Abbie decided to have a word with Sifton, and ran down the elegantly curved staircase, with the brass handrail worn smooth by generations of trailing fingers.

Sifton had apparently heard her light footfalls, for his tall, stately figure appeared like a genie from a small room near the door.

"May I help you—madam?" he inquired. The brief hesitation was due to deciding what title to confer on Miss Fairchild. The "madam" was not a slur on her age, but a compliment to her obviously genteel background. Not a mere governess, as he had feared, but a superior sort of impoverished lady.

"I believe gypsies are setting up camp on the estate, Sifton," she said. "Is her ladyship aware of it?"

"It is not gypsies, madam. Her ladyship is aware of the campers. His lordship wrote her a note requesting her to make the folks welcome."

"But who are they?"

His distaste was evident. "It is O'Leary's Circus, madam. A traveling horse show with acrobats, music, dancing animals, and so on. Her ladyship was not aware of it when she invited Lady Susan and her friends."

"Oh, dear! How long are they staying?"

"A week."

"Then, they will be here for our entire visit. I wonder what I ought to do."

"Perhaps inform Miss Slatkin—and meanwhile,

we shall keep a tight watch on the young ladies." His sympathetic eye reinforced the suggestion that he would aid her in this difficult task.

As they spoke, an echo of drumbeats came wafting through the grand hall. "That will be the performers arriving now," he said. "I believe they march through town to incite interest for the show. Her ladyship has been eagerly awaiting them." He bowed and left.

Abbie stood a moment with her head whirling. She must notify Miss Slatkin at once! The visit would be terminated. She would not get to see the da Vinci cartoons. Severely as she felt the loss, she could not face a week of trying to control the girls—Kate in particular—with a bunch of rowdy circus folks less than a mile away. But could the girls return to school? The staff were all away on holiday. Miss Slatkin had spoken of painting the bedchambers. Oh, dear!

As she stood, thinking, Lady Penfel came bustling into the hall. "What fun!" she cried, and hastened to the front door, her bronze head bobbing in excitement. Over her shoulder she called to Abbie, "Call the girls, Miss Fairly. They will not want to miss this."

It was not necessary to call them. Kate and Annabelle had heard the drum and had come running, with Lady Susan following at a more sedate gait. Her haughty face was in contrast to the other girls' excitement.

"What luck!" Kate exclaimed. "I feared we would be dull as ditch water in the country, but a circus! That is something I like!"

It was hard to deny them a look at the parade when their hostess stood at the doorway, urging them out. Truth to tell, Abbie felt a surge of excitement herself at the insistent beat of the drum. A brown mongrel of no identifiable breed appeared at her skirt tails, barking furiously. They went in a troupe across the sun-dappled lawn to a lane leading to the meadow where the tents were already under construction. Servants ran out to join them as the motley parade passed, accompanied by the ragtag and bobtail of village youngsters.

A covered wagon led the way, with "O'Leary's Traveling Circus" painted on the canvas side in glaring red, enlivened with details of the show. "Dancing girls, tumblers, elephants, performing horses, monkeys." In the driver's seat sat a handsome young fellow with a bold smile and flashing eyes. His outfit resembled the scarlet regimentals of an army officer, liberally trimmed with brass buttons and gold braid. In place of a shako, he wore a red-peaked cap trimmed in gilt. He lifted his cap to the ladies, revealing a head of glossy black hair, and called a greeting as he passed.

Abbie noticed with a sinking heart that Kate waved back frantically, Annabelle stared in fascination, and even Lady Susan evinced some interest, which was unusual for her. But the most excited of them all was Lady Penfel.

"What fun!" she cried. "I wish Algie were here. How he would love it. Oh, look, Cuddles! A mama elephant and her baby."

Abbie looked to see if Lady Penfel was addressing her stately butler in this familiar fashion, and realized it was to the mutt that she spoke. Cuddles barked his agreement and went running after the parade, tail wagging in delight.

Lady Penfel turned to Sifton and asked, "Where is Algie? I wonder why he is not here for this show."

"His lordship is at Lewes, your ladyship."

"So he is. I had forgotten. Wretched how things slip out of your mind when you are old. He went to offer for Lady Eleanor. Surely, she will not have him, do you think?" Before Sifton could reply, she turned her attention back to the parade. A flat-bottomed carriage came into view. On its floor three young ladies in immodest outfits of vaguely Egyptian style undulated to raucous music provided by the marching band.

"How do they do it?" Lady Penfel asked. "Only look how they swing their rumps. Their bones must be made of rubber." She tried to imitate them, gave a wince of pain, and grabbed at her back.

The dancing girls were followed by donkeys decked out in bells and ribbons and hats, and by tumblers and jugglers in motley suits. These bold fellows leered at the female servants and called out, urging them to attend the grand opening that night.

Lady Penfel turned to Abbie. "I have free tickets for us all. Algie sent them," she said, with the air of conferring a great treat.

"Oh, I am not at all sure Miss Slatkin would—"

"Deuce take Miss Slatkin. The ladies are under *my* care!" In the twinkling of a bedpost, the foolish-looking woman turned into a grande dame. "I would not dream of depriving them of such a rare treat. Where else will they see dancing dogs and such sights? Marvelous. I can hardly wait."

Abbie stood, disliking what she was hearing, but forbidden by both etiquette and orders from disagreeing with her hostess. Miss Slatkin had made perfectly clear she was to defer to Lady Penfel's decisions, but Miss Slatkin was not personally acquainted with the dowager. Until that moment, Abbie had not realized the full difficulty of her position. She had no real authority over the girls, but if they came to grief, she would certainly be held responsible.

"It is your decision, ma'am," she said, loud and clear.

"Of course it is, Miss Fairheart."

As the last of the parade disappeared behind the house, Lady Penfel turned a severe eye on Miss Fairchild. "I do hope you are not one of those schoolmistressy sort of schoolmistresses, Miss Fairwell. You are much too young to be so stiff-rumped. Algie would not like it. His papa, now, that was a different kettle of fish. I was never allowed to have any fun when he was alive. I was too busy giving him three daughters before I finally had a brace of sons—an heir and a spare. Then my job was over. But now that I have got the girls bounced off and buried Penfel," she said with relish, "I can do just as I like. Algie does not mind what I do, so long as I do not wear red shoes or go to the cent-per-centers. Ladies do not wear red shoes."

Miss Fairchild was only half listening. The other half of her interest was on the raddled face of Lady Penfel. What an intriguing character for a portrait! Like something out of the *Rake's Progress*, but in lieu of decrepit, penurious, defeated old age, it was imperious old age in a silken gown, with all the fire and spirit of youth still burning brightly.

A hand spotted with liver marks and flashing two large diamond rings clutched her arm. "I believe I threw my hip out with that wiggling," she said, laughing. "Give me a hand into the house, will you, dear?" They began the walk to the door. "So how are

19

you going on? Sifton is taking care of you? Good," she said, before any reply could be made.

"We'll have tea, then we can take the girls down to watch the performers set up their show before dinner. They don't get to see such sights as that in London, eh?"

"Actually, Miss Slatkin's Academy is at Maidstone." Abbie felt a pronounced compulsion to object to something, and she had already learned that her hostess would not be talked out of any opportunity for impropriety.

"So it is. One forgets things in old age. Not that I am old!" she added hastily. "How old do you think I am? The truth, now."

Abbie did some hasty calculations. Three daughters, then two sons. Susan had mentioned Lord Penfel was thirty. "It is difficult to say. In your—er, early sixties, perhaps?" she said, wanting to flatter the old lady. She looked eighty.

"Ha! I am seventy years old! But young at heart. Still young at heart." She inclined her head to Abbie and said, "I color my hair. Don't tell anyone! Not that it is white, but its red has faded. Just a little tint, for I cannot abide to wear a cap, and I like to look nice for Algie."

Abbie's poor opinion of Algie, otherwise known as Lord Penfel, lowered another notch. Bad enough that he refused a serious artist permission to view his precious treasures, but what sort of son encouraged his aged mama to make a spectacle of herself? What sort of gentleman invited a load of circus performers to his estate when schoolgirls were visiting?

Tea was served in the saloon. Lady Penfel was so invigorated by the arrival of the circus that she chattered like a monkey to the girls.

20

"Which of you is the brewer's gel?" she asked.

"That would be Miss Kirby," Lady Susan informed her, indicating Annabelle.

"Nettie tells me she hopes to land her for Sylvester. There is a match made in heaven. The brewer's gel will like to have a sort of handle to her name, and Sylvester likes his ale. But he has not gone to fat yet. Mind you, it won't be long the way he soaks it up."

"Nettie is my mama, the duchess," Lady Susan explained to the others.

"Aye, Nettie Carr did pretty well for herself, nabbing a duke, and she was nothing to look at, either. Looked quite like yourself, Susan. Mind you, Charles was downright ugly. No getting around it, he had a face like a bulldog. So fortunate you children favored Nettie in looks, Susan."

"Charles is my papa, the duke," Lady Susan added, ignoring the rest of the speech.

While Lady Penfel gorged herself on macaroons and tea, Lady Susan encouraged the others to try the bread and butter. When the tea was over, Lady Penfel rose and said, "And now we shall take a stroll down to the meadow to watch the performers." She winced when she tried to take a step.

"Fetch the dogcart, Sifton," she bellowed into the hallway. "This demmed hip is cutting up on me. Dance while you can, girls. Old age creeps up on you swiftly. I don't regret a single thing I ever did in my life, except perhaps marrying Penfel. What I regret is all the things I didn't do. You get your bonnet and come with me, Susan. The cart only holds two. The others can walk. They are young and supple. Miss Fairchild will see no harm comes to them." She inclined her head to Susan and said in a perfectly audible aside, "She is one of those schoolmistressy gels. Pity, for she ain't at all bad-looking. Not so pretty as the brewer's gel, but she has countenance."

As they went to fetch their bonnets, Kate lifted an eyebrow and said, "How do you like that assessment, Miss Fairchild?"

"At least she got my name right this time."

She studied her image as she adjusted her bonnet before her mirror. She did not think she looked so very schoolmistressy. Her high-poke bonnet of glazed straw was quite dashing, with a cluster of silk posies on the side. Her coiffure, perhaps, was a trifle quaint. She wore her chestnut hair pulled severely back from her face to appear older than her twenty years. Some of the senior girls were nearly seventeen. One wanted to look as old as possible, and with a clear, unlined face, a healthy complexion, and hazel eyes undimmed by age, it was not easy. Wearing dark colors of a severe cut helped. The suit she wore at the moment was a well-tailored navy serge. But schoolmistressy? None of Miss Slatkin's other mistresses wore such stylish gowns or carried such expensive reticules, or had such good gloves.

Perhaps it was her height that Lady Penfel found intimidating. Lady Penfel was not much over five feet, whereas Abbie was five feet and a half.

"Come along, Miss Fairchid. You look marvelous, as usual," Kate called from the doorway.

Annabelle gave a sweet, childish smile. "At the academy, we all think you are the prettiest mistress, Miss Fairchild," she said. "Kate was saying just last week that if you curled your hair and wore nice gowns, you might still find a husband. Weren't you, Kate?"

Kate lowered her brow at her friend. "What would

22

Miss Fairchild want with a husband?" she said. "She is an artist. They are unconventional. I expect she has a lover," she added daringly. "Eh, Miss Fairchild?"

"Certainly not!" Abbie said. She picked up a silk foulard, and tucked it into the neck of her suit to lessen its severity. Then she led them out the door, smiling softly to herself. A lover indeed! They would not have said anything so dashing about any of the other mistresses!

Chapter Four

Other than having to worry about the young ladies, Abbie thoroughly enjoyed the visit to the meadow. It felt good to stretch her legs in the fresh air and sunshine, with the unbounded view of greenery all around. Lady Susan was her least favorite of the girls, and she remained with Lady Penfel. Using Cuddles as an excuse, this noble pair roamed amid the tents, calling the dog's name and peering about, ogling the performers who ogled them.

Abbie kept Kate and Annabelle a few yards back from where the show was being prepared. It was a lively, noisy scene. Workmen in shirtsleeves were hammering the stage together. The air was punctuated with hammer blows, loud talking, laughter, and more than a little profanity. In one tent, women were making their toilette with the flap door wide open. Anyone could look in and see them in their chemises. Several village youngsters were doing so.

From the sidelines, Abbie and her charges watched jugglers practicing their art with orange balls, watched a man lead a huge black bear to a trough of water, and played with a white monkey who hopped right onto Kate's shoulder. It tried to pull a feather off her bonnet, until a young man came and led the animal away.

"There is the handsome one!" Kate exclaimed, clutching Annabelle's elbow.

Peering through the moving crowd, Abbie discerned the man who had been driving the wagon. The dark-haired, flashing-eyed man had changed out of his scarlet uniform into skintight buckskins and a white shirt, open at the throat, to show a triangle of tanned chest. She reluctantly admitted that he was indeed a handsome specimen of young manhood, though not the style she favored herself. There was too much of the strutting-cock walk to him. He was too aware of his own charms as he swaggered through the crowd of workers, giving orders, joking and patting the female performers here and there in a very familiar way.

Lady Penfel approached him and spoke to him in her friendly manner for a minute or two, probably asking if he had seen Cuddles. The charmer assumed a whole new expression when with ladies. Abbie watched him bow in deference to the countess and the duke's daughter. When they walked away, the man spoke to a few of his workmen and began looking about, presumably for the dog.

Kate's enticing smile soon drew him to the edge of the meadow. Abbie could hardly order the girls not to speak to him when they had just watched Lady Penfel and Susan do so, but she could keep a close watch to see no impropriety occurred.

He was wearing his deferential manner when he approached them, but she sensed from his dashing eyes, which he could not quite control, that he simply wanted an excuse to scrape an acquaintance with the girls.

25

Experience told O'Leary it was the older lady he must ingratiate. He bowed punctiliously to them all, but directed his words to Abbie.

"Good afternoon, ladies," he said. "I am O'Leary, the proprietor of this show. Lady Penfel has lost her dog and has asked me to look about for it. You haven't seen it?"

"I saw Cuddles over there," Kate said, pointing to the far side of the field. "I think someone was preparing food. A dog will always go after food, Mr. O'Leary."

"I see you are familiar with dogs, Miss—?"

"Fenshaw. And this is my friend, Miss Kirby, and our chaperon, Miss Fairchild."

His bow was a pattern card of grace. "Delighted to make your acquaintance, ladies." Sensing a stiffness in Abbie, he said, "Lady Penfel mentioned the young ladies were accompanied by a schoolmistress. Surely, you are too young to be playing propriety, Miss Fairchild?"

She refused to acknowledge the remark as a compliment. "I believe I am old enough to fulfill my duties."

A closer look at her glinting eyes and stiff expression decided him against this tack. He turned to Kate. "Where, exactly, did you see the dog, Miss Fenshaw?"

"There! There he is!" Annabelle cried. She took Kate's hand and drew her into the meadow, chasing after Cuddles. Mr. O'Leary gave Abbie an uncertain look, and followed the girls. After they had gone a few yards, Abbie lifted her skirts and went grumbling after them.

As she approached the tent where the female performers were arranging their toilettes, she heard a soft, masculine laugh within, followed by a giggle of

26

higher pitch. Without hearing a single word, she had a very good idea what was happening inside that tent. You would think they would close the flap at least. As she passed, a man ducked his head and came out of the tent.

"See you tonight then, love," a female called after him.

The man was just waving farewell when he spotted Abbie frowning at him. Her frown was originally caused by the couple's lechery. When she saw that the man was a gentleman, it deepened to a scowl. It didn't take some men long to sniff out a light-skirt. The circus was not even set up yet, and already this one was making his assignation for after the show.

He lifted his curled beaver, smiled, and said, "Good afternoon, ma'am."

After a moment's hesitation, she said, "Good day," in a curt voice, and hurried on.

The man followed close behind her. "Is there some trouble?" he asked. "You seem—harried." His voice was a well-modulated, deep drawl.

She stopped walking and turned to face him. She already had a general impression of a tall, well-built man in a blue jacket. On closer inspection, she noticed that the jacket was of finest Bath cloth, hugging a pair of broad shoulders. The cravat was immaculate and intricately arranged. A glint of gold at his waistcoat hinted at an expensive watch in his pocket. When he removed his curled beaver, his raven hair glinted with iridescence in the sunlight. Something in his general appearance reminded her of O'Leary. He had O'Leary's flashing eyes and encroaching manner, but a closer look showed her his eyes were a deep, huckleberry blue, while a certain stiffness, a sense of condescension, told her his social position was quite different from a circus manager's.

"There is no trouble, thank you."

"Then, I suggest you not linger about here. A circus under construction is no fit place for a lady—especially unchaperoned."

"Nor is the dancers' tent a fit place for a gentleman," she retorted, and brushed past him.

When she heard him following behind her, she felt a little thrill of triumph. Despite her plain suit and uncurled hair, this dasher was interested enough to follow her! He put his hand on her elbow and drew her to a halt. "I must take exception to that speech, miss! There are plenty of gentlemen loitering about the dancers' tent."

As she shook off his hand, she looked over his shoulder to the tent and replied with great condescension, "The ones peeking at the naked women are mostly ragged 'gentlemen' ten or twelve years of age."

"You are right to be annoyed with them. A gentleman of any age ought to see to his toilette before calling on a woman." She sniffed but did not deign to reply to this. "You must be a local lady," he said. "Do I know you?"

She turned and walked away. He followed. "Apparently, your circle of female acquaintances does not extend so far as Maidstone," she said.

A throaty chuckle came over her shoulder. "*Au contraire!* To Maidstone and considerably beyond, though I have not seen you there, or I would remember. So you are from Maidstone. Are you visiting locally?"

"In a manner of speaking," she replied vaguely, for to tell him she was visiting Penfel might give him

28

an unrealistic notion of her social status. She was only there as a working guest.

As they moved beyond the throng, he stepped up beside her and glanced down at her in a flirtatious manner. "But how intriguing! You must be visiting the vicar. I heard he had a niece visiting."

"Why do you think that?"

His bold eyes darted over her bonnet, her gown, and back up to her eyes. "An educated guess."

So that was his assessment of her toilette! Suitable for a vicar's niece. Well, at least he had not taken her for a schoolmistress. "No, I am not acquainted with the local vicar."

"Would your host be Mr. Rogers, the solicitor?" he ventured. She ignored him. "One more guess. One is always allowed three shots in the fairy tales. I have it! You are Sir Harry Felcombe's new governess!"

"Actually, I am a guest at Penfel Hall," she said, omitting "in a manner of speaking" this time.

His raised eyebrows suggested not only disbelief, but amusement. "The quality of guests at Penfel Hall has certainly improved since last I was there!"

She stopped and looked all around.

"What are you looking for?" he asked.

"A dog."

"Any particular dog, or do you merely have a fondness for strays?"

"An ugly brown mongrel, part hound." She spotted Kate and Annabelle, pulling Cuddles along by his collar. "Oh, there he is now!" she said, and ran off without looking back.

The gentleman smiled bemusedly, then his huckleberry eyes turned to examine Kate and Annabelle with the keenest interest. It promised to be an interesting visit.

Using the pretext of Cuddles's restlessness, Abbie eventually prevailed on Lady Penfel to return home, and take the girls with her. Only Lady Penfel rode in the dogcart; the others walked beside her. The talk was all of O'Leary, his handsome face, his manly physique, his friendly manner. Lady Penfel led the cheering section, which made discouraging this talk difficult.

"What I call a manly man," she said with obvious approval.

"Did you ever see such eyes?" Kate sighed.

Even Lady Susan joined in the chorus. "He is one of those irresistible rogues, quite like Byron's Corsair."

"We weren't allowed to read that!" Annabelle said.

"Papa, the duke, has a copy at Wycliffe" was Lady Susan's reply. There was no arguing with this. What was done at Wycliffe was above reproach.

"Byron! How I should love to meet him!" Lady Penfel cried. "Every lady ought to have one flirtation with a dasher like that."

Abbie had a fleeting recollection of the gentleman in the beautiful jacket. What would it be like to have a flirtation with him? She felt it would spoil her for more ordinary gentlemen.

Lady Penfel did have one last, regretful caution, however. "O'Leary would make an excellent flirt, but you must not go falling in love with him," she said.

Abbie's mouth fell open when Lady Susan said, "I disagree, Lady Penfel."

"You are quite right, Susan, as usual. Such a sensible gel. He is exactly the sort one should fall in love with, but not marry. Why should men have all the fun of lovers and we ladies have none? We ought to set up a petticoat rebellion."

When they reached Penfel, Miss Spadger, a stout woman of a certain age, had arrived and was unpacking for the ladies. Her hair was bound in such a tight knot on top of her head that it gave her slant eyes. She came to report to Abbie, whom she had known forever. Her sister worked for Colonel Fairchild, and Spadger occasionally gave them a hand when they were giving a party. She had already put an apron over her navy gown and a white cap over her brindle knob.

"May I have a word in private, Miss Fairchild?" she said, ushering Abbie into her chamber. "I hear there is a circus going on. That will not make your job easy, my dear. You want to keep an eye on Miss Fenshaw. She is up to every rig and racket in town. And poor Miss Kirby! She would be easy pickings for one of those wretched fellows. She hasn't the wits God gave a rabbit."

Abbie felt free to speak frankly to this old friend. "The deuce of it is, Lady Penfel has no more sense than Miss Kirby. She is positively encouraging the girls to make cakes of themselves. You must help me keep an eye on them, Spadger."

"Aye, and I want to see that show tonight as well. Sifton tells me they have all got tickets. But I'll see to the ladies' toilettes before I go, and be back in time to get them into their beds, never fear. You are to dine early, as the circus begins at seven. Now, what will you wear for dinner, dear?"

"The dark green gown, but I can take care of myself. You had best go to Lady Susan or she will be in the boughs."

Spadger went bustling out the door. Abbie put on

31

her dark green moire gown. It was simply cut to cling to her figure. As she prepared in front of the mirror, she thought it looked rather well with her chestnut hair and hazel eyes. Knowing she would be wearing a bonnet to the circus later, she left her hair in its usual simple arrangement. A bonnet would crush her coiffure if she tried anything fancy. Before leaving her room, she added her necklace, an antique chain of gold links with pendant flowers, set with emerald chips.

At five to seven, Abbie went to collect the girls, who had gathered in Lady Susan's chamber. They looked like a bouquet of spring flowers in their pastel gowns of modest design and their fresh faces. Young ladies were not allowed to display their shoulders at Miss Slatkin's Academy. That treat must wait until they made their debuts, but they were allowed to wear simple jewelry. Pearls were the favorite choice. Lady Susan's pearls, however, were allowed to boast a pear-shaped diamond pendant.

"I shall remove my jewelry before we go to the circus," she said. "You should all do the same, ladies. There are bound to be cutpurses there."

"Why can't we wear our jewelry, if it's only purses they cut?" Annabelle asked.

"It is not only purses they cut, Belle," Lady Susan explained. "They are common thieves."

"I should love to meet a cutpurse!" Kate said, smiling at such a delightful notion.

Abbie felt a sense of anticipation at the prospect of her first dinner in such a stately home as she led the girls down the gracefully curved staircase, with the marble floor gleaming below. The girandole overhead threw dancing diamond reflections on the marble. She envisaged a vast display of silver and crystal on the table, with footmen lurking at every shoulder and dainty dishes whose ingredients and manner of eating would be a mystery. What never occurred to her was that there would be anyone but themselves for dinner.

When she led the ladies into the saloon, she stopped and emitted an audible gasp. It was him! The lecher from the circus, sitting with Lady Penfel and making himself very much at home. He looked exquisite in a burgundy jacket, with a largish diamond pin sparkling amid the folds of his cravat. His jetty hair and swarthy complexion held some suggestion of the gypsy. Who could he be? She looked about, half fearing O'Leary would be lurking in some corner, but at least he was not there. When she returned her gaze to the stranger, he had lifted his quizzing glass and was studying the girls. As she looked, the glass turned in her direction and stopped.

"Surprise!" Lady Penfel cried, smiling from ear to ear, and looking more like a light-skirt than ever in a royal purple silk gown that displayed several inches of wrinkled chest that a large diamond necklace did not begin to conceal. "Algie has come home to see the circus."

Lord Penfel rose and bowed to the ladies. His laughing eyes turned to Miss Fairchild, the quizzing glass held in midair now. "I have been looking forward to this," he said. "The ladies were strangely reluctant to reveal their names in the meadow this afternoon. Now, which one, I wonder, can be the schoolmistress?"

"She is the old one," Annabelle said nodding at

33

Abbie. Kate pinched her. "Ouch! Oh, do I mean the older one? Older than us."

"Older than we," Lady Susan corrected her.

"Caparisons are odious, ladies," Lord Penfel chided, and redirected his gaze to Abbie.

Chapter Five

As they approached Lady Penfel, Abbie noticed two other young gentlemen standing by the closer fireplace, talking. One was still in his teens, to judge by his coltish appearance. He was tall and slender, all arms and legs and awkward movements. When he had outgrown his adolescence, he would be handsome. He had something of the look of Penfel around the eyes, and the same dark hair. The other was an older, altogether less prepossessing gentleman with blond hair. A pair of spectacles perched on the end of his nose lent him a bookish air, though his shoulders were broad. The two gentlemen stopped talking and turned to examine the ladies as they entered, then went forward to meet them.

Lady Susan was not tardy to put herself at the front of the line to greet her cousins. Always a demon for propriety, she greeted the older brother first. "Penfel," she said. "I had not heard you were to be here. I thought you were at Lewes. Is one to assume Lady Eleanor rejected your offer?"

Penfel's jaws worked in silent annoyance. "We found we did not suit. Kind of you to ask. Delightful to see you again, Susan." It did not help his mood when he noticed Miss Fairchild biting back a smile—

not of welcome, but of amusement at the public announcement of his jilting.

Penfel presented his brother, Lord John, and his tutor, Mr. Singleton, who was some tenuous relation, a second or third cousin.

Abbie stared to learn that this awkward young cousin was the man who had written so haughtily, denying her access to the da Vinci cartoons. She had pictured A. Singleton as an older, austere gentleman who delighted in thwarting her wishes. She had also understood he was Lord Penfel's secretary, but very likely he filled dual functions at the Hall.

"Johnnie will be going up to Oxford in the autumn," his proud mama announced. "If Singleton can ram Latin and Greek into his head," she added.

Lord John was smiling a bewitched smile in Kate Fenshaw's direction.

"Poor you!" Kate said to him. "I hate Latin and Greek worse than blood pudding."

Mr. Singleton made a demurring sound in his throat at this heresy. He was a better communicator with pen and paper than with the spoken word. When ladies were present, he did most of his communicating without actually opening his mouth. Once he had muttered, "Happy to make your acquaintance," he seemed to fall mute. It was a malady common to tutors and governesses when they were allowed into their employers' company for a purely social occasion.

"You seemed curious about our schoolmistress," Susan said to Penfel. She was a lady much burdened with facts, but not much attuned to people's feelings. She presented her school friends first, however, as she knew a schoolmistress was only a servant, whereas she and the students were well-dowered ladies. "And this is Miss Fairchild," she ended, nodding to Abbie.

"Fairchild?" he asked, frowning.

Abbie assumed his mama had used some other name. "Fairchild," she said, loud and clear.

He gazed into her eyes while a slow smile grew on his lips. "The sins of the parents ought not to be visited on the children—even those older than ten," he added, to remind her of their meeting at the tent. "I am not the one who called you Fairychild. You must not hold me to account for the misdeeds of others. No doubt I shall have plenty of my own to account for soon enough."

Abbie steeled herself against his insidious charm. "You need not feel any need to account to me. You are not one of my pupils."

"One never knows. We might teach one another something," he replied. "I have never been much good at writing, for instance. Singleton is kind enough to be my scribe." The words were innocent enough, but the mischief in his eyes left no doubt that he was flirting. Did he know she was the one who had written asking to see the cartoons? She was surprised he would remember her name. Abbie was not accustomed to flirting, certainly not in front of her girls, and especially not with such a dasher as Lord Penfel. With a warm flush rising up her throat to color her cheeks, she turned aside in confusion to speak to Kate.

"Let us eat," Lady Penfel said, giving her hand to Lord John to assist her from her comfortable seat. "We don't want to be late for the circus. I have not seen a circus since I sneaked out on Penfel and went to Astley's Circus in London. Goodness, it must be

37

more than a decade ago. How you loved the ladies in white face and short skirts, eh, Algie?"

"Ladies in any guise, especially short skirts," he murmured.

"And that funny little monkey, Jacko," Lord John said.

"And Grimaldi!" his mama cried, smiling in fond memory. "No, that was at Sadler's Wells. We took you lads for Johnnie's sixth birthday. How he had us roaring with laughter at his stunts."

"What stunts do you do, Lord John?" Annabelle asked.

Abbie noticed Penfel's eyebrows rise with interest as he studied Annabelle. He did not laugh at her; she sensed he was just interested in originals of any sort.

It was Kate who laughed. "Lady Penfel meant Grimaldi, Belle," she explained.

"Oh. Who is Grimaldi?"

"He was a clown," Lord John explained.

Lady Penfel went chattering toward the dining room. "I loathe all that precedence stuff and nonsense, wondering whether a duke's eldest son precedes an earl, and a duke's daughter a baroness. As to bishops! What a problem they are, so sensitive of their honors. A batch of schoolgirls will not care about all that stuff."

Lady Susan apparently cared. The duke's daughter glided forward and attached herself like a limpet to Penfel's arm for the trip along the corridor and around the corner to the table. Lord John latched on to Kate. Singleton's spectacles glinted in Abbie's direction. She pushed Annabelle forward and walked in last with Lady Penfel. Without waiting to be asked, Lady Susan took the place of honor at her host's right hand. By some silent ocular message, she indicated to Kate that she was to sit at Penfel's left hand. Lord John quickly took the seat beside Kate, and the others found places around the board, with their hostess at the foot of the table. Abbie sat beside Mr. Singleton, with Lady Penfel at her right hand.

The dinner table was not the opulent display Abbie had half feared and half hoped. In fact, the dining room was not at all grand, but a cozy room with an unfashionable hearth and a table that seated eight comfortably, and with squeezing might have accommodated ten. A simple bouquet of wildflowers formed the centerpiece. The array of knives and forks was only moderate, as was the meal. The simplicity of the arrangement was soon explained.

"Do you usually take dinner in the morning parlor, cousin?" Lady Susan asked Penfel.

"I didn't know Algie was coming," his mama replied from the foot of the table, making clear she did not consider the ladies alone enough reason to set up the grander dining room. "If I had known you were coming, Algie, I would have had a better dinner. For school chits, you know, it did not seem worthwhile ordering the fatted calf. We have just got our Metcalfe relatives blasted off. They were here for two weeks, and you know how they like to eat! You were not here to shoot any game for us. The chickens are decimated. Johnnie has put on a couple of pounds, and I feel like a Strasbourg goose myself. Cook did us proud. She deserves a rest."

Lady Penfel had met her match in outspokenness. "The dinner is not so bad as to require an apology, cousin," Lady Susan said. "At school, we are always served only one course and one remove.

I have eaten even tougher mutton than this at Miss Slatkin's."

"And at Wycliffe, if memory serves. Your mama sets a dreadful table." She shook her head and gave a tsk. "Poor Nettie. But then she was never trained to be a duchess. Such a wretched chore for her, trying to run a house the size of Wycliffe. It only encourages hangers-on, having a place the size of a hotel. For myself, I find fifty bedchambers sufficient."

"Really?" Susan said, surprised. "For small house parties, I daresay you manage. A duke, of course, entertains on a grand scale. Papa spoke of adding a wing after King George and Queen Charlotte stayed with us one autumn. We had a deal of other company—it was at the time of my brother, Lord Godfel's, marriage to Lady Sylvia Trane. Her papa is also a duke—a very suitable match in every way. Godfel, of course, is Papa's eldest son. Their majesties brought several of their children and fourteen servants, and stayed a month."

"Royal servants are more trouble than their masters," Lady Penfel scolded. "I did not find old Farmer George any trouble at all. He was as easily amused as a child, but those ladies-in-waiting! They were as proud as peacocks. Farmer George was a great help in the vegetable garden. I remember he and a couple of the princesses picked beans for our dinner one evening."

"Ah, that would be after he became mad," Susan said, and tackled another bite of the tough mutton.

The ladies from Miss Slatkin's were accustomed to Lady Susan, but being with new company made them aware of her unconscious rudeness. Abbie felt positively sorry for Penfel when she turned to him and asked in no quiet voice, "Why did Lady Eleanor turn you off, cousin? Was it because of your rackety reputation, or were your pockets to let?"

Penfel smiled blandly. "What a lack of imagination, Susan. There are other reasons."

She nodded, always happy to learn something new. "What are these other reasons?" She glanced at her hostess. "There is not insanity in the Penfel family, is there, ma'am?"

"Only a touch," she replied, then turned to her elder son. "I daresay you got too forward with Lady Eleanor, eh, Algie? She is one of those schoolmistressy gels who raises a hue and cry if a gentleman tries to snuggle her. Fancy a son of mine losing control with Eleanor Bagshot. It would be like kissing a cow. The Bagshots all have those great calf eyes and placid expressions."

"Was that it, lechery?" Susan asked Penfel.

"How are you liking school, Susan?" was his reply.

"Fine. You did not answer me, Penfel."

He gave her a haughty stare. "It is not only ladies who grow deaf when the conversation is unsuitable for mixed company. I wonder they do not teach manners at Miss Slatkin's Academy." He looked down the board, where Kate and Annabelle were snickering into their napkins, and Abbie was working heroically to dismember a piece of mutton from her chop. "What subject do you teach, Miss Fairchild?" he asked.

Abbie sensed the moment had come to broach the da Vinci cartoons. "I teach art," she said. "I have been to Penfel Hall three times before to admire your magnificent collection."

Mr. Singleton looked up and stared at her with dawning knowledge. He opened his mouth to speak, then closed it again.

41

Penfel and Abbie discussed art intelligently for a few moments, then she said, "I have never seen the da Vinci cartoons, as they are not on display. I am a great admirer of da Vinci. Would it be possible to see them?"

"I'll show them to you tomorrow," he replied promptly. "They're really marvelous, but perishing a little around the edges, you know, being so old. That is why they are not on display."

"Leonardo lived from the late fifteenth to early sixteenth century," Lady Susan informed them. "That would make the sketches three hundred years old. Naturally, it is one's duty to preserve such priceless treasures. Papa, the duke, feels the weight of responsibility in that respect. Wycliffe has so many irreplaceable artworks. He has seven Van Dycks at Wycliffe and three Rembrandts, along with many Italian masterpieces. Also a collection of Chinese jade, and a small golden epergne in the Blue Saloon, said to be the work of Bernini—he was an Italian sculptor of the seventeenth century. In the front hall, there is a quartet of life-size statues of the seasons by Canova. And in the—"

"Why do you not send us a catalog, dear?" Lady Penfel said.

"I would be very happy to, ma'am. I didn't know you were interested in art."

"I'm not."

Mr. Singleton made a choking sound in his throat. Abbie glanced at Penfel, and saw he was watching her closely, with an amused smile twitching his lips. He lifted his glass and made a silent toast in her direction. For that brief moment, she felt a special closeness to him, as if they two alone found this strange meal and strange collec-

42

tion of humanity interesting and amusing. It was not a cynical smile, but displayed a tolerant appreciation of foolishness. She felt an answering smile spread across her lips.

"Tell me about the show we shall be seeing tonight, Algie," Lady Penfel said, breaking the mood.

Lady Susan blinked once and returned her attention to her dinner. Penfel outlined some of the treats in store for them, and the remainder of the meal passed more lightly. Lady Susan was not allowed to collar the conversation again. As she was not much interested in learning about a circus, she ate instead. Kate was making great headway with Lord John. Once Mr. Singleton discovered Miss Kirby was as ignorant as a swan, he relaxed a little and managed a few questions.

"Ah, er, your papa?"

Strangely, Annabelle, who could usually misunderstand most things, seemed to understand his cryptic utterances.

"Kirby's ale," she replied. "Are you familiar with it, Mr. Singleton?"

"Excellent stuff. Prefer it to Whitbread's."

"Really? I shall tell Papa. Are you a teacher like Miss Fairchild?"

"That's it."

"You must be very smart."

"Not pretty, though, like—"

"No, handsome," Annabelle said. Singleton turned bright scarlet.

The gentlemen made short work of their port after dinner while the ladies went abovestairs to remove their jewelry and don their mantles. They were all soon back in the saloon, eager to attend the circus. With three gentlemen escorts, Abbie did

43

not think any harm could befall them. When they left, Lady Susan had a firm grip on Penfel's right arm, his mama on his left. Lord John offered Kate his arm, and Mr. Singleton, for the first time in his life, had the pleasure of escorting two pretty ladies out the door. Neither of them paid him the least heed. Abbie was too busy admiring Penfel's manly figure, and Annabelle's chatter was all about Lord John and Kate.

"I believe she has a *tendre* for him," she said, smiling at such romantical doings. "He is very handsome, is he not, Miss Fairchild?"

"Very handsome—and very young," Abbie replied.

A hum that might have been agreement or its opposite issued from Mr. Singleton's throat.

Abbie could not work up much interest in Kate's romance. As Penfel left, he had cast one rather wistful look in her direction, shrugged as though to say, "What can I do? I have been shanghaied." Then he said over his shoulder, "We shall have a good coze in the morning—about da Vinci." But his gleaming eyes did not speak of art.

She did not think again of her first meeting with him until they were actually at the circus ground, when the women's tent reminded her of it. He had been in that tent, flirting with the showgirls. He had made a date with one of them for later that same evening. He was a lecher—that was why Lady Eleanor had turned him off.

Abbie was determined to see those da Vinci cartoons, to copy them if possible, but she must be on her guard against their flirtatious owner, who could say more with his flashing eyes than most gentlemen could say with words. She sensed he had some interest in her, but common sense told her it could be nothing but a flirtation. But why should she not enjoy a flirtation with a handsome lord? As his own mama had said, why should gentlemen have all the fun and the ladies have none?

Chapter Six

Mr. O'Leary, back in his imitation of an army officer's uniform, welcomed the audience to O'Leary's Traveling Circus. The most eager face in the crowd was Lady Penfel's. Her party had choice seats in the first row of a raised platform that surrounded the central stage. She shrieked in glee when the horses, decked out in head feathers and gilded saddles, were trotted out and performed their tricks. The clowns, the dancing dogs, the bear who balanced a ball on the end of his nose—all were equally enjoyable to this indiscriminating lady, and indeed to her guests, for at Miss Slatkin's an evening out meant a dull concert of antique music or a lecture on history, philosophy, or morals. The dancing girls were particularly enjoyed by the gentlemen.

"I could do that!" Kate boasted, as the girls undulated to the accompaniment of violin and drum.

Lady Susan stared at her as if she had suggested she could dig a ditch. "Ladies do not perform for money," she said.

Lord John gave Kate a smile that held a shadow of his older brother's mischievous charm. "I promise not to pay you if you'd care to perform for us one evening."

Abbie was so well entertained by the show, she

didn't realize Lord Penfel had left until the intermission, when his mama demanded refreshment. He had sat on one side of Lady Penfel, Abbie on the other, so she had not had a direct view of him; but she had been anticipating the intermission when some rearrangement of the seating was possible, or at least some general conversation.

"Where has Algie gone?" his mama demanded. "Off chasing the girls, I warrant. Never can keep his hands off a pretty wench. He certainly did not inherit that from his papa. Say what you like about Penfel, he was no womanizer. He hated most women as much as he hated men. You will have to get us refreshment, Johnnie. Do they have any ices?"

"It is a little chilly for ices," he replied, and went after lemonade and gingerbread.

There was some moving about and changing of seats during the intermission. When they regrouped, Abbie found herself on the end of the row, with Mr. Singleton on one side and an empty seat on the other. Mr. Singleton's attention was riveted on Miss Kirby.

As enjoyable as the show was, Abbie felt some pleasure had gone out of the evening. She wondered which one of the dancers Penfel was meeting. The saucy redhead, the voluptuous blond, or the vivacious brunet? Still, it was a salutary lesson for her. She meant no more to him than these circus girls. She would bear it in mind next time he tried his flirting tricks. As if fate were determined to put her to the test, he immediately appeared in the empty chair by her side.

"What have I missed?" he asked.

She quelled down her pleasure and replied, "Lemonade and gingerbread."

"Thank God for small mercies. I have been having a word with O'Leary."

She gave him a knowing smile. "I see."

"No, really!" He uttered a nervous laugh. "Where did you think I had gone?"

"I hadn't noticed you were missing, until your mama began looking for you."

"I see I have made a powerful impression on you! O'Leary wanted to purchase oats and hay from me for his horses," he said. "I had had a word with my groom, and was arranging the transfer of the feed."

"I have already told you once, Lord Penfel, you need not account to me for your deeds."

"This sounds like a friendship made in heaven. A beautiful young lady who has a sense of humor, some conversation, and demands no accounting for one's misdeeds."

She noticed the subtle shift from deeds to misdeeds, but didn't think Penfel was aware of it. He had been doing something he oughtn't, and the word had slipped out unheeded. "Do you usually feel obliged to account to virtual strangers for your behavior, milord?"

"No, no. I am not so scrupulous as that. Only to charming schoolmistresses who are staying under my roof. One would not like to have his romantic career bruited about Miss Slatkin's. All the best debs are nurtured there."

"They would be disappointed to hear your notion of romance is feeding horses," she replied. When a quick frown drew his eyebrows together, she said, "That is what you were doing, was it not, arranging feed for the horses?" Her cynical smile made a jest of the question.

Penfel lowered his head and peered at her from

48

below his eyelashes. "Hoist by my own petard, I believe, is the expression called for here."

Abbie realized this was not the sort of conversation she ought to be having with her host, and determined to raise the tone. "About the da Vincis, Lord Penfel, when might I—"

"Well done, ma'am!" he said, and clamped her on the arm. "A quick change of subject is the best slap on the wrist when a gent has allowed the conversation to wander into forbidden purlieus. You seem mighty interested in da Vinci."

"Yes, I am," she said, edging her arm free.

"I think you are very unambitious to settle for a gent who has been dead these three hundred years."

"Not at all. I appreciate maturity in a gentleman."

"A skeleton would be a nice quiet companion as well. Not given to foolish chatter, like some we could mention, eh, Miss Fairchild? You should really thank me, you know."

"So I shall, once I have been allowed to see the sketches."

"I mean for delaying the pleasure for you. You, if memory serves, have been chasing after them for some time?"

"Yes, I wrote to you on two different occasions."

"Anticipation increases the pleasure. In fact, anticipation is often the greater part of the pleasure." His voice lowered as he spoke. The way he looked at her, with warmth in his lingering smile, suggested he was not speaking of the chase of anything but women. "It has been my experience that the thrill of the chase often exceeds the capture."

"That must depend on what, or whom, one is chasing. I cannot believe Leonardo da Vinci will be a disappointment."

49

"I don't know about that. That is a very equivocal smile the Mona Lisa wears. I believe she was bored to tears before he had finished taking her likeness. Nor is there any mention of his ever having won a wife."

"I am not pursuing the cartoons with any hope of marrying their creator. I just want to study them, and perhaps try my hand at copying them, if you would allow it. It is only by trying to imitate that one becomes aware of her own shortcomings. Da Vinci's pictures, even his cartoons, live. When you look into the eyes of his creations, you almost feel you know his sitter. His line is so sure, his shading is exquisite—it's marvelous."

As she spoke, his eyes flickered over her animated face. One hand came out, as if to touch her cheek, but he withdrew it when she pulled back.

"I forgot myself," he apologized. "It was da Vinci's ugly old men you were speaking of, not the sparkling eyes and exquisite lines of Miss Fairchild."

"Ugly!" she exclaimed. "They are beautiful!"

"No, no, you were supposed to simper and protest that I call you beautiful."

She was glad of the darkness, which concealed her flush of pleasure. "You are perfectly absurd!"

"I must disagree. Lady Susan is perfectly absurd. I may criticize her as I am her cousin, and she never hesitates to give me a thumping set-down. I am imperfectly absurd. I have moments when I am completely rational. When we come to know each other better, you will agree with me."

"Lady Susan is always rational, if somewhat outspoken."

"There is a piece of understatement if I ever heard one. Somewhat outspoken, indeed! While we are having a good gossip, tell me, what do you know of the young lady John is making a cake of himself over? It runs in the family," he added, with a glinting smile that suggested he knew he was making a cake of himself over her, and enjoying it very much.

Abbie had never met anyone like him. Her few suitors had been such dull worthies as a vicar, an aging major who visited her papa, and a cousin who had a smallish estate in Somerset. She knew she was completely out of her depth with this handsome, practiced Lothario, and renewed her efforts to keep the conversation within the bounds of propriety.

"Miss Fenshaw comes from the west of England. Her papa owns a coal mine. She is well behaved, has a dot of twenty thousand, and is the most popular lady in the school."

"No ill to say of her, eh? I find that curious. No one is all sweetness and light."

"She does not do well at her lessons, not through any mental deficiency, but due to a lack of effort."

"Does she have any conversation beyond hating things and loving them?"

"Certainly she has. Sometimes she varies her talk by saying she does not give a hoot about something."

"And the blond?"

"Miss Kirby's papa owns Kirby Brewing."

"That explains Susan's interest in the chit. Is it Tony or Sylvester she plans to give Miss Kirby to?"

"Lord Sylvester."

"Poor Miss Kirby."

"Poor Sylvester," she replied, then gave a gasp as she realized she had sunk again into such frankness with her host.

He smiled a charming smile that sent shivers down her spine. His eyes, in the shadows, glittered like black diamonds. "You were kind enough to tell me I need not account to you for my shortcomings. I can only reciprocate. I shan't tell Miss Slatkin how barbarously you denigrate your charges. She's a pretty little widgeon, Miss Kirby."

"Yes, and sweet-tempered."

"I shall have a dancing party to allow her to meet some gentlemen. And we shan't invite Lord Sylvester, even though he is visiting only ten miles away."

"Is he? Lady Susan did not mention it."

He inclined his head to hers in a conspiratorial manner, and whispered, "There is a good reason for it. You must not say a word, but—" Then he stopped and peered all around for spies. She looked at him, with her eyes wide open. "The awful truth is, he is visiting commoners. Not a title to their name! Plain Mr. Sheridan is his host. But we shan't mention it."

A gurgle of laughter caught in her throat. "You are really too absurd," she chided. "I thought you were going to say he was a thief or a murderer or a lecher."

"I see lechery is last on your list of evils. That, being my own sin, is encouraging."

She remembered, then, Lord Penfel's lechery, and drew herself up sharp. How had she allowed herself to sink into such familiarity with this acknowledged rake? "I am astonished that you, who claim to know so much about women, don't realize that for us, lechery is a man's worst sin. Ladies can tolerate other deficiencies of character, but that one puts a man beyond the pale. No one loves a lecher for long."

Penfel heard the genuine anger in her voice and blinked in astonishment, wondering how this delightful little flirtation had suddenly turned into a lecture. He had thoroughly enjoyed Miss Fairchild's efforts to resist his charm. He had met these straitlaced ladies before, and knew just how to handle them. But he had no notion how to handle a schoolmistress who looked at him as if he were a worm.

"I don't claim to know so much about women," he said. "It is their infinite variety that intrigues me." He had never met one before who cut up at him in the middle of a flirtation. "I know virtually nothing of you, for instance. Who and what is Miss Fairchild? Other than being a schoolmistress with a strange passion for Leonardo da Vinci, I mean?"

"She is an orphan now, but you must not pity her on that account. She has no memory of her papa, for she was only six when he died, and she was already grown up when her mama passed away three years ago. I went to live with my paternal uncle in Maidstone, who neither beats nor starves me nor forces me to work my fingers to the bone for my daily bread. I teach because I enjoy the change. Getting out of the house, you know, and meeting people. I am what is called a day teacher. I return home at night."

"And your uncle—is he married, by the by?"

"He is a widower, with no children. I suppose one could say I am like a daughter to him. He was a colonel with the army in India. He does very little entertaining—he is getting on in years now. His main interest is the battle of Mysore, in which he played some part."

"And proses your poor ears off with a recital of it, to judge by the edge of ennui that has crept into your voice. At least I hope it is not my own conversation that has caused it."

"Oh, no!" She was surprised at how easy he was to talk to, as if he really cared about her dull life. In many ways, she was fortunate. More so than the other teachers, who were her closest friends. One could hardly complain to them, but she did have her burdens to bear, and it helped to be able to discuss them with someone who was sympathetic. She was surprised, too, at his understanding, the quick sympathy that glowed a moment in his eyes, and softened his expression to tenderness. "And what of Lord Penfel? Who and what is he?"

He lifted his hands, palms out. "Just what you see. A spoiled elder son of whom little good can be said, except that he has never knowingly harmed anyone, male or female. A somewhat negative virtue, though I do try to retain some semblance of chivalry toward the fair sex in particular."

In a good mood with him, she said, "That is better than a vice, at any rate."

Then she turned her gaze to the stage. A new act was just beginning, featuring the white monkey, who always did exactly the opposite of what his master commanded. If the man in the shiny black suit said, "Sit!" the monkey stood up. When the man played on his concertina and said, "Dance," the monkey sat down and covered a yawn with his hand. When the man said, "Bad Mojo," the monkey struck his master a blow on the cheek. The crowd was vastly amused. Abbie did not smile, but sat in

54

a bemused state. She was acutely aware of Penfel sitting beside her, watching her from the corner of his eye.

Midway through the act he leaned toward her again. "If this is how you are going to behave, ignoring me for a monkey, I shall leave. So there!" he added, to make perfectly clear he was joking. "John and Singleton will see you home. I have some business with O'Leary."

"A dancing lesson, perhaps?" she asked, with a knowing smile.

"Ah, you did hear me this afternoon. I had hoped— No matter. I shan't be long. I am a fair to middling dancer already."

"Practice makes perfect."

"These accusations of perfection are all unwarranted, ma'am. Fair to middling is what I said. I'll be back at the house before you retire."

"I mean to see the girls have an early night."

A sly smile lit his eyes. "Then, you are not interested in a quick glance at the da Vincis? I had thought I might show you where they are kept, and give you the key so you could get an early start on your copying in the morning." He watched, chewing a smile as she bit her lip in indecision. Then he laughed. "I shan't be late. My 'dancing lesson' won't take a moment. I'm a fast learner, am I not?"

She knew exactly what he meant. He had learned how to bear lead her. The da Vincis were his strong suit, and he meant to play it for all it was worth.

"Could your mama not give me the key?" she asked.

"I dare not entrust such priceless objects to her. She would stick a pin in one and hang it in the

55

kitchen to be splattered with grease. And how would I make Miss Fairchild dance to my tune without them?"

He rose, waved, and sauntered off, not toward O'Leary's covered wagon, but toward the dancing girls' tent. He had still not returned at the show's end. Lord John and Mr. Singleton saw the ladies home.

"That was dandy," Lady Penfel said, smiling from ear to ear. "I shall go to see the show again before they leave. Where would one get a monkey, Johnnie? Such jolly company. Cuddles will be green with envy. Serve him right for running off on me."

"P'raps O'Leary could tell us," Lord John replied.

"I shall ask Algie to arrange it. It need not be a white monkey. That would be hard to keep clean. Well, shall we have tea before retiring?"

A great silver tea tray holding sandwiches and a plum cake was brought to the saloon. While they ate, there was some discussion of what the girls should do on the morrow. Abbie mentioned the tour of the gallery and an art lesson.

"Save that for the afternoon," Lady Penfel said. "Tomorrow morning will be fine, whatever of the afternoon. Red sky at night, sailors' delight. There was a red sunset. That means fair weather in the morning. Get out and enjoy the morning. Go riding or for a drive or for a walk about the estate. You and Singleton must take the ladies into the village one day, Johnnie. Young gels always like rooting about the shops."

The ladies and Lord John gave enthusiastic vocal agreement, and Mr. Singleton hummed his. Abbie foresaw she would not be required to chaperon the girls when they had two male escorts. She would be free to wander the gallery and work on the

56

da Vincis. She kept an eye on the longcase clock in the corner as it ticked off the minutes, wondering if Penfel would return before they retired. He had said he would not be long, but already he had been gone the better part of an hour. It was half past ten. The young ladies usually retired at ten.

The tea was drunk, the plum cake and sandwiches eaten, and still he had not come.

"It is time for bed, ladies," she said, rising and thanking their hostess.

As they left the saloon, the front door opened, and Lord Penfel stepped in. His questioning glance flew to Abbie. "Not retiring so soon?" he asked.

"It is going on eleven," she replied stiffly.

"I was detained longer than I had hoped."

Lady Susan left the group and went toward Penfel. "Your mama was saying we ought to go out tomorrow morning, Penfel. I thought you might show me about the estate. I could ride your mama's mount."

"Perhaps Johnnie could show you. I am pretty busy at the present time, Susan."

"The next day will do as well," she said, and returned to the group.

Penfel just shook his head and said to Abbie, "I'll just get you the key to the art room for those cartoons you wished to see." He bowed to the girls. "Good night, ladies. Sleep tight."

Abbie hesitated a moment, caught between excitement and an urge to give Penfel a set-down. That confident face suddenly annoyed her. It would not do to let him know how badly she wanted to see those da Vincis. What this rogue really wanted was to get her alone in the art room, and she feared she was not up to the challenge of controlling him.

"Tomorrow will be fine, Lord Penfel. Thank you,"

57

she said. Then she turned back to the girls and led them abovestairs, gloating over the shocked expression she had glimpsed on Lord Penfel's handsome face.

The girls were chattering among themselves as they climbed the stairs.

Kate said to Annabelle, "I wouldn't encourage Mr. Singleton too much if I were you, Belle. He is only a tutor, you know."

"I think he's sweet."

"He is perfectly harmless," Lady Susan said. "Lady Penfel said we should all enjoy a flirtation."

"I doubt it is only a flirtation you have in mind with Lord Penfel," Kate said. "I noticed you pitching yourself at him."

"I have been thinking about why he came back to Penfel Hall just now. I daresay he has decided to offer for me. Until I hear from Papa, I shan't discourage him entirely."

When Abbie was tucked in her bed, her mind roamed over the doings of her unusual day. It was mostly of Penfel that she thought, wondering at his apparent interest in her, when there were younger, prettier ladies with fat dowries in his house. She did not think he was interested in Susan, though Susan did have some interest in attaching him, if her papa wished it.

Was that why he was making his preference for herself fairly obvious, to discourage Susan? He said he never intentionally harmed anyone, male or female. Was this little flirtation designed to show Susan he was not interested in her, to save her embarrassment and perhaps even heartbreak? If so, that was very considerate of Susan, but what of herself? Did he think she didn't have any feelings? That because she was older and a schoolmistress, she was

58

sensible enough to realize nothing could come of their flirtation?

This seemed eminently logical, but unfortunately, the human heart was not ruled by logic. There was danger to ladies in this theory of petticoat rebellion.

Chapter Seven

The ladies from Miss Slatkin's were accustomed to rising early. At seven-thirty the next morning, Abbie was dressed and ready for the day. She went to see that Spadger was up and about to give the ladies a hand with their toilettes. She found her with Lady Susan, who always expected the lion's share of attention. Susan stood with her arms out while Spadger slid a deep blue jacket on her and buttoned it. Then she handed Spadger the brush, sat in front of the mirror, and waited for her hair to be attended to.

Spadger glanced up from her brushing and said to Abbie, "I was just telling her ladyship she ought to make a play for Lord Penfel. Ever so handsome, isn't he? And rich as a nabob as well, to judge by this house. Of course he ain't a duke, but then there's more dukes' daughters than dukes, so her ladyship here won't have an easy time nabbing one of them great gaffers."

Lady Susan studied her reflection in the mirror and said pensively, as if talking to herself, "He is the Earl of Penfel, also Baron Rutcliffe, and perhaps Viscount Chance—he is presently heir to his uncle Worley's earldom, though Worley might yet produce a son. As well as Penfel Hall and his London house and a hunting box in the Cotswolds, he has the Rutcliffe estate, in Cornwall. I would certainly accept an offer, were it not for Lady Eleanor's turning him off. I fear Papa might think it would look odd for the Duke of Wycliffe's daughter to accept the leavings of an earl's daughter. Other than that, Penfel is one of the prime *partis* on the market. Very likely I shall accept him."

"If he offers, that is to say," Spadger added.

"Of course," Lady Susan agreed, unoffended. "I wonder why Eleanor jilted him."

"Outrun the grocer. Pockets to let—temporary like—that's what I think," Spadger said. "I heard belowstairs he's only let O'Leary put on his show here for the hundred pounds rent it put in his pocket."

"That is entirely possible," Lady Susan said. "The late Lord Penfel did lose heavily upon 'Change."

Abbie knew she should not gossip, but with the excuse of looking out for her charge's interest, she said, "Surely, it is his lechery that makes him ineligible?"

"He is not really a lecher," Lady Susan said. "A flirt, of course, but then he is so rich and handsome that all the ladies flirt with him. It is a sort of defense. My oldest brother, Lord Godfel, was the same when he was a bachelor. He is Papa's heir, you know, so all the ladies were running after him before he married Lady Sylvia Trane. By flirting with them all, he prevented any particular one from thinking she had the inner track."

"That's clever, then," Spadger said.

Abbie said nothing, but she noticed that this would explain why Penfel had struck up a flirtation with herself, as she had surmised last night.

"Yes," Lady Susan agreed, "but there is no getting around Lady Eleanor's having turned Penfel off, and she, you know, is only the Peevey's third daughter, with ten thousand dowry. And she is not so very pretty, either. I made sure she would have him, for Penfel is a close friend of her brother, Oliver, and the whole family. He spends considerable time visiting at Lewes."

"It's a caution," Spadger said, and put down the brush. "There we are, then, milady." Lady Susan nodded her satisfaction, but did not think to thank Spadger.

Abbie went to see to her other charges. Annabelle sought her advice on what gown she should wear for the morning outing. "Now that I'm away from Slats, I can dress a little more stylishly."

"What have you brought that you don't wear at Miss Slatkin's?"

"Nothing," she said. "But if I had something more dashing, I could wear it."

"Oh, yes."

They decided on a mauve suit. Kate beckoned Abbie into her room as she left Annabelle's.

"Miss Fairchild, you sly rogue!" she said. "Lord Penfel has a *tendre* for you! Is it not exciting? If you marry him and I marry Lord John, we would be sisters-in-law! I should love it of all things."

Abbie just smiled at her wild imaginings. "It is a little early for you to be speaking of marrying Lord John, Miss Fenshaw. You have not known him for twenty-four hours, and you are only sixteen besides."

"Have you never heard of love at first sight, Miss Fairchild?"

"I have read of it in books of fiction."

"My mama married at sixteen. Of course Papa was older. Lord John is going on eighteen."

"Do you know whether he has an estate, or what his fortune is?"

"I don't give a hoot about that!"

"He has not even begun university yet. It will be years before he thinks of settling down."

"Oh, I hate being young! I wish I were old, like you. You could marry Lord Penfel tomorrow."

"Only if he asked me," she said, and soon left, nursing that thoughtless "old, like you."

Spadger cornered her for "a word in private" before she went belowstairs. "You will have to keep an eye on Miss Fenshaw and Lord John, to see they don't run amok, for if Lord John is as big a flirt as his brother, there could be trouble brewing in that corner."

"I am quite aware of it, Spadger."

While they spoke of Lord John, it was the image of Penfel's handsome, laughing face that loomed large in Abbie's thoughts. Too large! She must not let herself become infatuated with him. Lady Susan claimed he was no lecher, but she had not heard the way he laughed with the dancer in the tent. It would keep her busy, overseeing all her charges, with very little help from their hostess.

At eight o'clock, the ladies were at the table for breakfast. Neither Lady Penfel nor her elder son was there, but Lord John and his tutor were waiting for them. Lord John promptly showed Kate to a chair beside him. When Mr. Singleton cast a shy smile on Annabelle and made some incoherent sound as he drew a chair for her beside himself, Abbie began to fear she might have another romance to worry about. And to add to her troubles, Lady Susan looked definitely put out that Lord Penfel was not there to court her.

No audible conversation occurred between Singleton and Annabelle, but at breakfast's end, he appeared to have offered to show the ladies about the estate, along with Lord John. Lady Susan announced that she would play propriety to allow Miss Fairchild to enjoy the gallery without feeling she was abandoning her duties. After a moment's consideration, Abbie agreed. The girls considered Lady Susan second only to Slats as a chaperon, and Slats was second only to God. Abbie's hope was that Lord Penfel would give her the key to the art room.

As she would be giving the girls a tour and dissertation that afternoon, or in the near future at least, she decided to try her hand at copying the Chardin that morning. She brought down her painting materials and easel, and found her way along various marble corridors to the gallery.

Sunlight slanted through tall mullioned windows along one wall of the long hall. Down its center, the parquet floor wore a long blue runner patterned with red flowers and arabesques. Between the windows hung paintings of Penfel ancestors in historical costumes going back for centuries. Brass and marble statues on pedestals varied the decor. The unwindowed wall held a more diverse collection of larger paintings—Flemish, Italian, and French, some of them huge enough to fill a whole wall of a small chamber. They were fine paintings by famous names, but Abbie had lost interest in overly large historical scenes depicting masses of humanity in classical poses. They were too old and too academic for her more modern taste. Da Vinci had never bothered with these grandiose monstrosities. She found more art in a simple Madonna and child than in all of Rubens's posturings.

64

Portraiture was her true love. She borrowed a chair from beneath one of the windows and set up her easel in front of the simple Chardin genre painting of the *Girl with Rose*. The long stretch of empty corridor was silent and eerie. No echo from the busier part of the large house reached her. She might have been alone in the world. The only moving thing was the dust motes floating desultorily in the shafts of sunlight from the windows.

She took up her pencil and began sketching the outline of the girl. She was perhaps twelve or thirteen, just at that age where a child becomes a woman. Her brown hair, lightened to blond where the light struck it, was looped high on her head, showing her clean young profile. Marvelous how Chardin had expressed her tender yearning in profile, when one could not see her eyes, or much of her smile. The rose, perhaps, was a symbol of her beauty and innocence. Faces were easy for Abbie. The rose and the girl's hand more difficult.

Time flew when she was at her easel. She did a quick sketch, then began applying the pigment. An hour passed, another thirty minutes, and the girl's face and hands were completed to her satisfaction. The rose in her hand, the gown and the background were still to be done. The eerie feeling faded as she concentrated on her work. She began to paint in the girl's blue gown. From time to time she glanced to the door from the main hallway, thinking Lord Penfel might seek her out. She had mixed emotions about meeting him again. She was as eager as ever to see the da Vinci cartoons, but she felt some reluctance to cross swords with the flirtatious Lord Penfel. Even then, she admitted to herself, there was a good deal of anticipation mixed with the reluctance. When was she ever likely to meet such a dasher again? "The twelfth of never," as her uncle would say, whatever that meant.

Engrossed in her work, she did not hear the soft footfalls on the carpet. Until a shadow fell across her canvas, she did not realize she had company. She looked up, startled and confused, and saw a man peering over her shoulder. She had been expecting Lord Penfel, and the gentleman had some resemblance to him. He was tall, with dark hair, and wore a well-cut blue jacket. It was not an old one, either. The cuffs were neither shiny nor frayed. It was the jacket that caused her confusion, for the last time she had seen Mr. O'Leary, he had been wearing his scarlet uniform.

"Good morning, ma'am," he said, smiling and making a graceful bow.

"Good morning," she replied, nodding.

"That's a nice picture you're doing there," he said. A slight lilt of Irish brogue made his speech attractive.

"Thank you."

"Not minding the school chits today, Miss Fairchild? I mistook you for one of them when I first glimpsed you from the doorway." Some trace of laughter in his eyes told her he knew perfectly well who he had come to talk to. It was an oblique compliment, perhaps, a hint that she looked younger than her years.

"Perhaps it is time I began wearing a cap," she replied.

"Nay, 'twould be a shame to cover those pretty curls. They glint like copper in the sunlight."

She just smiled without replying, and wondered what a circus manager was doing, running tame at Penfel. He could hardly be on such terms of intimacy with the owner that he was a welcome visitor.

"Were you at the show last night?" he asked.

66

"Yes, we all went. It was very amusing."

" 'Tis a tawdry thing, but my own. Since I lost my estate at the card table, I am left to shift for myself in the cruel world. But I shall gain no sympathy from a schoolmistress. Your lot is not an easy one. I've tried teaching youngsters myself."

His accent was good, and his easy manner suggested he had seen better days. The career he had chosen was strange, even infra-dig, but at least he worked for a living. She was ready for a break from her work, and set down her brush to show she welcomed the diversion.

She did not go into details about her own teaching, but said, "You are from Ireland, Mr. O'Leary?"

"That's right. Was it my name or the brogue that tipped you off?"

"Both."

"I'm from God's country, county Wessex. Have you been there at all?"

"No, I should like to go sometime."

"You've been to Italy, I expect? That is where you *artistes* go first."

"No, how I should love to! I've never had the opportunity to travel."

"It's very expensive."

"Yes, there's the rub, but of course there is a good deal of art from all over the world in England."

"Oh, aye, the English have always been good at plundering their conquests. Those who have the art don't appreciate it, though."

"And are not eager to share it with those who do," she added, thinking of her fruitless letters to Lord Penfel.

He began to talk about Ireland in a fond, reminiscent way, with his full share of Irish blarney. He was

67

an amusing rattle. Abbie found herself telling him something about her background. Like Penfel, he was understanding and sympathetic. Even more so, as his experiences were closer to her own. Of course, being a man, he had more freedom.

After a little conversation, he said, "But I'm keeping you from your work. I'd best be off. I came for a word with Penfel, but it seems the lazy hound is still abed. Nice to be rich, eh?"

"Very nice, I should think."

"Teaching's a hard game. You cannot have been at it long, Miss Fairchild. You haven't the hagged look of the professional scold."

"This is my second year."

"Could you not make a living at that?" he asked, indicating her canvas.

"Hardly. Being a lady makes it difficult to be taken seriously."

He hesitated a moment, then seemed to make his decision. He leaned a little closer to her and said, "What do you do with your pictures when you've finished with them?"

"When I am lucky, I sell them. More usually, I keep them. I have quite a collection in the attic at home."

"I could find a buyer for that one, if you're interested. We split the profit, fifty-fifty."

"That would hardly be worth your while, Mr. O'Leary."

He looked surprised. "I wager I could get you a couple of hundred for that Chardin. I know a fellow who collects French pictures."

She was surprised that he recognized the artist, but then his conversation had suggested he came from a good background. "But this is not a Chardin. It's just a copy."

His easy smile assumed a wolfish look. "I know that, you know it, but my friend don't know it." Then he gave a knowing little laugh. "What he doesn't know won't hurt him or us, eh? The risk would be mine. I'd not involve you at all."

"Are you suggesting to sell it as a Chardin?" she asked, hardly believing her ears.

"Why not? How much would you get for a Fairchild?"

"But that's against the law!"

He laughed at her naïveté. "I didn't make the law, nor did you. 'Twas made by the fine lords to keep the likes of you and me down."

She pokered up. "I don't believe we have anything more to say to each other, Mr. O'Leary," she said, and picked up her brush.

"Suit yourself, my dear," he said, and sauntered off down the long corridor as if he owned the place.

Really, the man was incorrigible! Whatever made him think she was a crook? She had let him think her circumstances were a little worse than they were, and from there he had leapt to the conclusion she would sell forgeries to better it. It is what happens when you let circus people onto your property. She ought to warn Lord Penfel. The man was as likely as not to stuff some valuable small item into his pocket. When she tried to continue her work, she found her concentration was broken and decided to see if Lord Penfel was about. She would warn him of O'Leary's criminal tendency—and hopefully get the key to the da Vinci cartoons as well.

She passed an open door on her way back to the main hallway. From it issued O'Leary's lilting voice.

"I've come about tonight, Penfel. We have a little game on after the show. 'Twill give you a chance to win back the blunt you lost last time."

"Excellent!" Penfel said, in the accents of an old friend.

The door closed, and Abbie stood, wondering what she ought to do. Very likely O'Leary was a Captain Sharp along with the rest. He had spoken of Penfel winning back the blunt, so clearly Penfel had already lost money to the rogue. When the conversation behind the door settled down to a friendly, conversational hum that suggested it might go on for some time, Abbie went up to her room. She would return a little later, after O'Leary had left, and caution Lord Penfel to be on his guard.

Chapter Eight

After stowing away her painting equipment, Abbie glanced from her window and saw Mr. O'Leary striding toward the fairgrounds. His broad shoulders and swaggering gait suggested he was the lord of the manor. Lord John, Singleton, and the young ladies, their tour of the estate having ended up at the circus, were strolling toward him in the sunlit meadow. O'Leary stopped to chat with them. Abbie watched as he lifted his hat and bowed all around. After a moment, the two young couples continued their walk. Lady Susan remained behind, talking to O'Leary.

Of course it was impossible to know what words were exchanged, but O'Leary's gestures suggested flirtation. He cocked his head aside playfully, he inclined his upper body toward Lady Susan's in the posture of romance. At one point, he reached out his hand and touched her arm. And Susan seemed less stiff than usual, too. It was unlike her to waste time on a commoner, but she stayed with O'Leary for two or three minutes. Abbie was just beginning to worry when O'Leary bowed, and Lady Susan hurried on to catch up to the others.

Selling a forged painting was bad enough, but setting up a flirtation with the Duke of Wycliffe's daughter could lead to something a good deal more serious. Lady Susan had a good notion of her own worth, but she was only sixteen years old. She would never have met anyone like O'Leary before. Such a practiced flirt might manage to turn her head, to compromise her in some manner. Abbie, who was considerably older than Susan, had fallen under his spell for a few minutes in the gallery. She must warn Lady Susan—and she must have that word with Penfel at once.

She immediately went belowstairs, where she found him in his oak-lined study, poring over a stack of journals at a handsome desk the size of a dining-room table. In this impressive setting and at this unexceptionable pastime, with a frown pleating his brow, Penfel seemed a more serious gentleman than she had been imagining. For the first time since she had met him, he appeared to be engaged in work. He looked as the lord of such a fine estate as Penfel Hall should look.

He glanced up when she entered, and the little frown eased to a smile. His eyes brightened perceptibly.

"Miss Fairchild," he said, rising and making a modest bow. "I need not ask to what I owe the honor of this visit," he said playfully. "It is not eagerness to see my poor self, but the Leonardos that have brought you knocking on my door. Come in, come in—as the spider said to the fly."

She was a little vexed that his seriousness had dissipated at the first sign of a female. "I am eager to see the cartoons, but in fact, I have come on another matter. A more serious matter altogether."

He waved a graceful hand toward the chair by his desk. She perched on its edge and leaned toward him as he resumed his seat. "I have come about Mr. O'Leary," she said.

His eyes opened wider. Again that frown grew between his eyebrows. "He hasn't been harassing you?" he asked sharply.

"In a manner of speaking, he has."

"What happened?"

"I was in the long gallery, copying the Chardin. O'Leary stopped for a chat."

Penfel's jaw tightened. He gave a tsk of annoyance and said, "Next time, you must have a footman with you. The gallery is not within shouting distance of the butler."

"You misunderstand, milord. He was not harassing me in a—a physical way."

"He didn't try to molest you?"

"No, I would not have minded that. That is—" She colored up as she realized her words were capable of misinterpretation. "I could have handled that," she modified. "My meaning is that the man is a crook. He offered to sell the copy I was making, try to pass it off as an original Chardin to what he called a friend of his. Some friend! He wanted to sell the man a forgery, for a couple of hundred pounds!"

Penfel considered this a moment, then said, unexpectedly, "It must have been an excellent copy."

"That is not the point! The man is a crook."

"And a rash one, to suggest chicanery to a young lady of impeccable morals."

"He was at pains to cozen me first. He was sympathizing with my hard life, to sound me out. He learned how eager I am to go to Italy to view the famous masterpieces there."

"You never mentioned that to me!"

"That is neither here nor there. We discussed how expensive travel is. Impossible really, and how those who have fine art don't appreciate it."

73

"I wonder what name arose in that respect?"

"We didn't mention names. I had no idea what he was up to, but I wager it was my complaints that made him think I could be corrupted. And this wretch is running tame at Penfel. I would not be a bit surprised if he picked up an expensive trinket or two before he left."

"He called to see me on business. I would hardly call it running tame."

"What was he doing in the gallery? He had no business there. You said yourself it is well separated from the part of the house where the servants are working. As he seems to be interested in art, he might very well be looking around with a view to robbing you."

His lips clenched together. "Thank you for notifying me. Is there anything else?"

Penfel made a show of concern, but some sixth sense told Abbie she had made no impression whatsoever. She trusted her next statement would open up his eyes.

"Yes. I saw him from my window just now. He was walking back to the fair. He stopped Lady Susan and talked to her for quite two or three minutes."

"Was she not with John and Singleton?"

"They walked on with the other girls. Lady Susan was alone with him. He was flirting with her."

Penfel shrugged his broad shoulders, like a man who couldn't—or wouldn't—take responsibility for grave matters. "No accounting for taste. I hardly see what harm could come to her during a few moments' chat, on my property, with John a few feet away."

"Lady Susan—all the girls—are just at that vulnerable age where their minds are full of men, yet they have no real experience of them. Lady Susan might very well find a rogue like O'Leary attractive. She has already been singing his praises."

The only emotion she could read was impatience. "The girls are in your charge. You must keep an eye on them," he said.

"You should not allow him to run tame about the estate when you are entertaining schoolgirls."

"The arrangement with O'Leary was made some time ago. I could not break the contract without being liable for his lost revenue."

Abbie's patience was growing quite as short as Penfel's. "Then, why on earth did you agree to let the girls come here?" she demanded.

"The question is why Mama let any of you come!" he shot back. "If it was an attempt to see me shackled to a stiff-rumped lady, it will not fadge."

Abbie emitted a gasp of astonishment. As Lord Penfel's fiery gaze was aimed at her, she felt for a fleeting moment it was herself he meant by the stiff-rumped lady. Their eyes locked in combat, then a slow smile crept across his face. When he spoke, his voice was burred with innuendo. "Lady Susan is not to my taste. If she were a charming artist, it might be quite a different matter."

Abbie felt the full force of that devastating smile. It was the eyes that were so disarming. They seemed to see through her skull to her mind, to her heart. She was thrown into confusion, and answered gruffly, "I'm sure the Earl of Penfel, Baron Rutcliffe, and quasi-Viscount Worley would be eager to catch such a prize as a penniless schoolmistress."

His eyebrows rose, giving him a quizzical air. "You are well-informed of my honors!"

"I certainly know more about you now than when

75

I left Miss Slatkin's, or I would not have agreed to come."

He refused to acknowledge this set-down. "The redoubtable Miss Fairchild bested by a circus manager? I am disappointed in you, ma'am. I made sure any lady who rode herd on a school of excitable young ladies, their heads full of romance, could tame a whole pride of lions if she set her mind to it. I shall misquote Plato and say, 'Of all the animals, the young lady is the most unmanageable.' "

"I would have to disagree with you, milord. Plato was right. The other sex takes the palm in unmanageability, especially when the gentleman has been been reared to think himself accountable to no one."

The corners of his lips quirked, and his dark eyes stared commandingly into hers. "You are speaking of Mr. O'Leary, of course—if you hope to see those cartoons."

She managed to reply in a tone of gentle irony that concealed her agitation, but made her meaning perfectly clear. "Of course. About the key—"

Penfel assumed a face of mock chagrin. "Do you know, I cannot seem to find it? It is not on my key ring." He drew out his heavy key ring and shook it, as if that proved anything. "I have asked Sifton to check his keys, and the housekeeper. No doubt it will turn up soon—" His eyes gazed deeply into hers, "If Miss Fairchild behaves herself."

Abbie's nostrils thinned in disgust. It was his petty revenge for her having dared to upbraid him.

She rose stiffly and said in her most severe voice, "Miss Fairchild has only been doing her job. If it amuses you to keep your little treasures horded away from the eyes of those who would appreciate them more than you do yourself, that is your concern."

He rose and accompanied her to the doorway. With his hand on the knob, he allowed his bold eyes to make a perusal of her high-necked gown. "Well put, ma'am. I have often said the same thing—to prudish ladies."

As his meaning sunk in, Abbie uttered a little gasp of shock at his gall. "I trust you do not speak in this lascivious manner to the girls," she said.

His dark eyes gazed unblinkingly into hers, until she felt mesmerized. "In case you have failed to observe it, I am not a boy; I am a man. I am not attracted to girls, but to women—like you." As he spoke, he put one arm around her waist and pulled her against him. His head came down, and before she knew what he was about, his hot lips had seized hers in a scorching kiss.

It happened so quickly, so unexpectedly, that she hadn't time to escape. When she pushed at his shoulders, his other arm went around her and she was locked against him. Her immediate reaction was outrage, tinged with disbelief. This couldn't be happening! But it was—that rock-hard chest, those strong arms, were all too real. She struggled, then before the embrace degenerated into a wrestling match, he released her. Without thinking of the consequences, she raised her hand and slapped his cheek with all the force she could muster in a confined corner. The echo of it reverberated in the closed room.

He didn't look shocked, or even offended, but only sheepish. "What, no 'how dare you?' " he said.

"I leave the banalities to you, milord. Now, if you would step aside, I should like to leave."

For one dreadful moment, she feared he was not going to let her, but after an instant, he stood aside

77

and held the door open. "What did you think would happen to the fly, when she came calling on the spider?" he asked, trying for an air of lightness.

This attempt at levity won him a cool glance as she sailed out the door with her cheeks flaming, and went to meet her young charges as they came in. She took a moment to collect herself before going to the hall, where she could hear their voices. She was so overwrought she feared the girls would know what had happened. Her hands were trembling, her cheeks were fevered, and her lips felt as if they were on fire. How dare he do such a thing, treat her like one of those light-skirts at the circus? Yet at the bottom of her heart, there was some tingling satisfaction. He would not have done it if he had not found her attractive. She took three deep breaths and continued on her way.

After greeting her charges, Abbie got Lady Susan aside and inquired what O'Leary had been saying to her.

"He asked me if Penfel was not the most beautiful house I had ever seen. I told him I found Wycliffe lovelier, and even Elmgrove superior in certain aspects. He was not aware I was His Grace's daughter."

But the wretch was aware of it now, and God only knew what he would do with such dangerous knowledge.

"You don't want to have anything to do with that man, Lady Susan."

"No, of course not, but one must be courteous to strangers. We know no ill of him, after all."

"I have good reason to believe O'Leary is a scoundrel, Lady Susan. I do not want you to speak to him again."

"He has the definite aroma of a fortune hunter,"

78

she replied. "I thought him brash and too forth-coming by half. When he hinted he would like me to meet him at the fairgrounds this afternoon, I told him ladies did not make assignations with circus managers. He is so determined he did not even take it as a set-down, but smiled and said he looked forward to seeing me again under properly supervised conditions. Quite incorrigible!" But her cheeks were pink with excitement, and her eyes bright with triumph.

He had obviously been plying her with compliments, and this was probably the first time any man had ever done so. Lady Susan may say all the right things, but she was secretly flattered at the handsome rogue's attentions, as any normal schoolgirl might be.

"We must warn the others," Abbie said.

"You may be sure I have done so, Miss Fairchild, but do add your cautions to mine. Such an irresistible rogue as O'Leary would have easy pickings of someone like Annabelle. Perhaps a word to Penfel—"

"Speak to him, by all means. He might listen to you."

"I'll have a word after luncheon."

Lady Susan went directly abovestairs to tidy up for luncheon.

Spadger was bustling about from room to room, making sure the young ladies had what they required for their toilettes. When she spotted Abbie, she came rushing forward, her eyes bright with news.

"Might I have a word in private, Miss Fairchild?"

"Certainly, Spadger. Come into my room."

There was nothing dearer to Spadger's heart than "a word in private." It might be a missing glove, a sandwich found in a girl's room (snacks in the room were forbidden at Miss Slatkin's as they were a lure to vermin), or the earth-shattering news that Miss Spadger would be half an hour late on the morrow, due to some family emergency.

On this occasion, her news was more weighty. She shoved a journal under Abbie's nose and said, "Just you have a read of this, Miss Fairchild!"

Abbie read: "Bow Street has been alerted to a string of house robberies that occurred during the past month in Kent and East Sussex. Silver, jewelry, and paintings were taken." It went on to name the victims and the specific objects that were stolen. It was the last name on the list that made Abbie's heart leap in her chest.

"Lord Peevey, of Lewes, lost a pair of Van Dycks, silver place settings for twenty-four, and an emerald ring of fifteen carats, set all around with diamonds, that Lady Peevey had removed and set aside on an end table in the saloon. It is believed the thieves gained entrance to the house in the afternoon while the family and servants were honoring the annual public day at Peevey Castle. The library door had been forced open. No items were removed from the upstairs, where the fabulous Peevey jewelry collection was kept in a safe.

"On each occasion, the O'Leary circus was performing in the vicinity. Last spring a similar series of robberies occurred in and around Birmingham, where a circus was also traveling. On that occasion, it was Brannigan's Circus. Bow Street is looking into the possibility of a connection between the two circuses. It is believed an employee of Brannigan's may have moved to O'Leary's show. Mr. Townsend, of Bow Street, has also suggested that Brannigan and O'Leary might be one and the same man. Bow Street can find no trace of Brannigan, but his physical description matches that of O'Leary. Bow Street is following the case."

"Lewes, you see! That is near where O'Leary had his last show," Spadger said.

"Good God! I wager that is where O'Leary latched on to Lord Penfel. He was at Lewes, trying to talk Lady Eleanor into marrying him."

"And now O'Leary is here, planning to rob the Penfels. You must warn them, milady."

"This should make Penfel open up his eyes!" Abbie declared, and rushed downstairs with the journal.

The calamitous journal article knocked her earlier visit to Penfel's study out of her mind. Until she was halfway down the stairs, she didn't realize that this meant another visit to his study. No, she would not enter this time. She would ask him to step out into the corridor. Indeed, having to face him at all would be embarrassing in the extreme, yet this was too important to ignore. He must be told, and at once.

Chapter Nine

Abbie caught Penfel just as he was leaving his office. He glanced at the journal she was carrying and without the necessity of speech, opened the door to usher her inside.

"I would prefer to talk in some more public place," she said coolly.

That sheepish look was back on his face. "Shall we take a spin into the village?" he suggested.

"I meant some more public room here at the Hall, as you very well know."

"And I know why, too, but you must not expect to be ravished every time you call on me, ma'am. You have had your little treat for today."

Before she issued the angry retort that was building, he continued in a more serious vein. "I am indeed sorry for my farouche behavior earlier, Miss Fairchild. I promise I shan't molest you this time. We can go to the saloon, where we will be overheard by half the household, or be semiprivate here, with the door open. Come, don't be foolish. I am not a hardened rake, I promise you."

It seemed petty to refuse. One little kiss was hardly sufficient to treat him like a criminal after all. She allowed herself to be ushered in, and took care to see the door was left open.

On his desk sat a journal he had been perusing, opened at an article dealing with the circus story.

"You have seen it!" she said.

"O'Leary brought it to me. He has assured me he is not and never has been Mr. Brannigan." His wafting hand indicated the chair by his desk. She ignored it.

"You can't take the word of that scoundrel. That robbery at Lord Peevey's estate two weeks ago—"

"Because O'Leary happened to be in the vicinity is not to say he is the thief. That is post hoc arguing, ma'am. I expected better logic of a schoolmistress— and more charity toward mankind than to rush about accusing a man only because he was in a position to do wrong."

Abbie was doubly distressed—a strike at her mind and her morals seemed like overreacting. "It is what Bow Street says," she pointed out.

"It is what Bow Street thinks. That unruly pack of scavengers are only after the reward money. O'Leary tells me he hired a juggler from Brannigan's Circus a few weeks ago. We believe he is the culprit. O'Leary turned him off when he read this."

"Why did he not turn him over to the constable?"

"Because he had no proof. As you are disturbed, I shall keep an eye on O'Leary. And will you please sit down? Your standing requires that I stand as well."

"I am only staying a moment," she said, but she sat down. "I hope your naive trust in mankind does not lead to disappointment. What you ought to keep an eye on is your house. I have no doubt—that is, I suspect he was examining the house for an easy means of entry this morning when he chanced across me in the gallery."

"My valuable items are insured."

Abbie regarded Penfel through narrowed eyes.

Charity toward his fellowman, indeed! Penfel was up to all the rigs. A man in his position would not be so naïve as he would have her believe. Why was he trying to con her? "I see your trust in mankind has not led you to omit more practical considerations," she said.

He answered blandly, "The jewelry, the silver, the paintings, the objets d'art, have all been insured since my papa's time. My man of business tells me I must keep up the payments."

"That only ensures monetary reimbursement, however. Some things are irreplaceable," she said, thinking of the da Vinci cartoons. "Did you not have any concern at allowing O'Leary to bring his show here when you must have known of Lord Peevey's loss?"

"Peevey did advise me against it. The fact is, I signed the contract with O'Leary before that robbery. As the deed is done, the best thing is to be quiet about it. No need to frighten your charges. The less talk there is, the more chance Bow Street has of catching the thieves, whoever they may be. I know how young ladies love to chatter. I hope you will not mention it."

"I am hardly a young lady."

"Surely, a schoolmistress is a lady!"

She glared. "I meant I am not young."

"I, being an ancient thirty, take leave to disagree with that, but I know what you meant."

"Then, why—"

A smile touched the corners of his lips. "You are endeavoring to teach me responsibility. I am trying to teach you not to be so serious—to joke, even flirt a little."

"I do not consider an unwarranted physical attack

84

flirtation." She glanced to the door to make sure it had not swung closed.

"It is still open. I haven't left my chair," he said. "Now, where were we? Ah, yes, we were discussing our harmless little flirtation."

"If you knew how disinterested I am in setting up a flirtation at this time, you would not speak so foolishly."

He nodded his understanding in a grave manner, then spoiled it by saying, "What time would be more convenient for you, ma'am?"

"Any time—after I have seen the da Vinci cartoons," she retaliated.

"At least I am good for something. But how do I hold your interest once you have seen the cartoons?"

"Does your great faith in mankind not include womankind, milord? Just because I will then be in a position to send you to Jericho does not mean I shall do so."

"It don't guarantee you won't. Unfortunately, we have some evidence, your charity does not match my own. I am speaking of your denigration of O'Leary," he added. "But, as a matter of fact, you are also demmed reluctant to flirt."

Abbie was not so unnatural as to dislike flirting with a handsome young buck, but their ideas of flirtation were at startling odds. She also felt his timing could hardly be worse. There were serious matters to be discussed.

"Have you never before met a lady who finds you resistible?" she asked grumpily.

"I have met several who said so. A feigned indifference, nay, even annoyance at a gentleman's advances, is the second most common way of engaging a man's interest. I have never met a woman who

85

meant it when she glared and lifted her nose in the air. Nor one with such a powerful right hand." He rubbed his cheek and directed a mock scowl at her.

"Well, there is a first time for everything. And now, if we are through with this pointless conversation, I must return to my charges."

"Are you not curious to hear ladies' most favorite manner of engaging a gentleman's interest?"

"Not particularly, but as you obviously wish to tell me, go ahead. It might be amusing to hear what you think," she allowed.

"With that passionate encouragement, how can I refuse?" He leaned toward her and said in a conspiratorial manner, as if he were sharing a secret, "Some ladies smile, and endeavor to make themselves agreeable."

"Do you know, it has been my experience that that is exactly how most gentlemen behave. It is— interesting to meet the exception. Making yourself agreeable is obviously not your strong suit."

"It is true, we Penfels like a good argument," he replied, refusing to take umbrage.

"Then, I must compliment you, milord. You have a positive knack for getting what you like." She rose and turned toward the door.

Penfel followed her. "Let me set your mind at rest with regard to O'Leary, Miss Fairchild. I shall keep my eyes open. I think he is guilty of no more than using shaved cards. I mean to examine the cards closely tonight."

"You will still play with him, knowing that?"

"I don't know it, any more than you know he is a thief." He stood gazing down at her with his hand on the knob of the open door, while his body blocked passage. "Have the girls told you what sort of party they would like? You recall I promised to have a party for them while they are here. Let us make it soon."

"Tomorrow evening would be fine. They enjoy dancing."

"And does Miss Fairchild also enjoy dancing?"

"Yes, of course. Who does not? They have been taking lessons for some time now, and are occasionally allowed out to a well-chaperoned party."

"Miss Fairchild providing the chaperonage?"

"Oh, no. I do not do that sort of thing. Usually," she added, as this seemed to make her presence in his house questionable.

He drew his face into a frown. "I wonder what urged you to take on the job this time?" She just stared at him, waiting. "You refuse to humor me? You are quite right. We have milked the da Vinci's dry of humor. That being the case, I have good news for you, Miss Fairchild. I have found the missing key"—a smile of pure delight lit her eyes—"and shall give it to you after luncheon."

He watched as her smile congealed to annoyance. "I would not want to ruin your lunch by causing too much excitement. Bad for the digestion, so my old nanny used to tell me. But, then, she also told me I would have curly hair if I ate up all my bread crusts, so I ate them dutifully, and have no curls despite my efforts."

His rakish gaze moved slowly over a few curled tendrils that had escaped Abbie's knot. "Do you attribute your lovely curls to bread crusts, ma'am?"

"I attribute them, when I want curls, to the papers I put in my hair at night. It is not fitting for a schoolmistress to encourage ignorant superstition in her charges."

87

"And your rose-petal complexion is due to liberal doses of Gowland's lotion, no doubt?" he said, struggling to chew back a smile.

"That, and using a parasol when I go into the sunlight. And you may attribute the fact that I am still here, listening to this nonsense, to the fact that you are blocking the door. Would it be too farouche of me to scramble out the window?"

The smile he had been fighting broke then. "You and I have enjoyed enough faroucheness for one day. We do not want to scandalize your charges." His twinkling eyes were a reminder of her former visit. Before she made a reply, he stepped aside and she sailed out the door, unmolested and telling herself she was happy for it.

Breathless with agitation at her latest bout with Penfel, it did not occur to her for quite ten minutes that O'Leary had not been carrying a journal when he was in the art gallery. He had gone from there directly to Penfel's study. She had seen no journals along the way. They were left in a stack on a table in the front hall. How had O'Leary got hold of the journal? Or was Lord Penfel not telling her the truth? It was difficult to believe that such an out-and-outer as Penfel would be so naïve as to trust a man Bow Street all but called a thief.

She found it hard to concentrate when Kate told her how fascinating she found Lord John, and how Mr. Singleton had a great *tendre* for Annabelle.

"How could you tell?" she asked.

"He spoke, Miss Fairchild. He said actual words. He said he found Kirby's ale smoother than Whitbread's brew."

"Very romantic. If you hear him mutter the word 'elope,' pray inform me and I shall speak to him."

"Oh, he is not that type, nor is John. Susan tries to hide it, but she is jealous as a green cow that we have both found a beau and she hasn't."

"I only hope she doesn't take it into her head to turn O'Leary into one. Let me know if he speaks to her again," Abbie said, and ushered the girls down to luncheon.

It was a lively meal, with so many romances percolating. Mr. Singleton was not driven to speak, but his eyes seldom left Annabelle. When Annabelle saw him sprinkling sugar on his ham, she wordlessly reached out and took the spoon from him. A soft crooning in her swain's throat was his only vocal acknowledgment, but his glazed eyes spoke whole volumes of poetry.

Lady Penfel had read the tale of O'Leary/Brannigan in the *Morning Observer* and was delighted at the notion of a criminal in their midst.

"We must go back to the circus this afternoon and try to ferret out some clues, Algie," she said. "You must be on intimate terms with one of the dancers by now. See what you can weasel out of her. Give her a trinket—but nothing too valuable, of course."

When Abbie glanced to Penfel to see how he reacted to this public announcement of his philandering, he was looking at her with a penetrating gaze. He gave her a long, slow smile that started at the corners of his lips and spread until his eyes were laughing. She noticed he did not try to bam his mama about O'Leary being innocent.

"Really, Mama!" he said, feigning severity. "What will the young ladies think of me?"

"Don't worry about that, Algie. Young ladies like a rake, always have, always will. They are fool enough to think they can reform him, but they can't."

89

When Abbie glanced at Penfel again, she saw his attention was directed to his plate. She thought he looked a little pink around the ears.

His mama continued, "Your papa had many faults, but he was not a rake. He might have been more likable if he were. Rakes like women. Penfel didn't. There was no fun in him. It was always hectoring and complaining. A gentleman don't complain about a thing if he can't change it. He was just a mouth atop a stomach."

Lady Susan looked up and said, "I am surprised you and he did not get along better, cousin, for it is said that birds of a feather flock together. But, then, it is also a truism that opposites attract."

A profound silence fell on the table. Mr. Singleton made a choking sound in his throat. The others were suddenly very busy with their knives and forks.

Lady Penfel sat silent a moment, then said mildly, "The thing about me and Penfel, you see, Susan, is that I let him quell my spirit from the start, for I was only a youngster, and he was more than a decade older than I. I did not stand up to him as I ought in the early days. It is more difficult later on. Remember that, ladies. Start as you mean to go on."

"Excellent advice," Penfel said, in a seemingly offhand manner, but Abbie wondered if it was meant for approval of her slapping him.

"Lady Susan will have no trouble," his mama continued. "Indeed, all of you seem pretty well able to look after yourselves. The gels are headstrong nowadays, as they should be." She looked around the board, then shook her head. "I see you glaring at me, Johnnie, thinking I am giving your little friend a disgust of you. Nothing I say applies to my boys. They are unexceptionable. I kept my mouth shut for the twenty-five

90

years I was a wife. If I don't talk now, when will I ever do it? Pass the mustard, Mr. Singleton."

Mr. Singleton passed the mustard, and the conversation turned to the dancing party.

As they left the dining room, Lady Penfel took Abbie's elbow and drew her aside. "I know you want to get the gels into the gallery for a lesson, Miss Fairchild. This afternoon is the time to do it. I plan to have Johnnie take me to the circus to snoop around and see what I can discover. We won't want the gels underfoot. They might give the show away. Such fun!"

She went twittering off abovestairs to prepare for her outing, and Abbie took the young ladies to the gallery. Mr. Singleton accompanied them, hovering at Annabelle's shoulder like a shadow. Inspired by her presence, he uttered a few words. "Pretty," he murmured in front of an Italian painting of a madonna. "Looks like you, Miss Kirby."

Abbie kept looking to the doorway, hoping Lord Penfel would bring her the cherished key, but after half an hour she gave up. Perhaps he had gone to the circus to give a trinket to his dancing girl. She wondered if the girl was smiling and making herself agreeable, and told herself the burning in her chest was disgust for Penfel's wretched morals. But at least he was ashamed of his behavior to a lady. And he had not lifted a finger to repeat it during the whole of her second visit to his study. She felt a wistful sense of regret that the incipient flirtation had not blossomed into something more. Perhaps a slap had been too great a reaction to a little kiss.

Chapter Ten

The young ladies proved to be about as interested in art as in the construction of a drawbridge. They yawned as Miss Fairchild pointed out the mastery of Van Dyck's portraits, the chiaroscuro of Caravaggio, the bravura design of Rubens, the sheer magical artistry of Rembrandt. Their notion of art appreciation was to spy out a resemblance to some acquaintance in every face, or a fault in the model's features, or clothing, or lack of it.

"What a horrid long nose the Penfels had in those days" was Kate's admiration of the Van Dyck of an early Lord of Penfel.

Even Lady Susan failed her. "When in doubt as to the country of origin of the artist, one has only to look at the nose," she informed them. "All the Flemish subjects appear to have noses like parsnips. It has often been remarked upon at Wycliffe."

"That lady with her hair falling down looks quite like my Aunt Lavinia. How fat the ladies are!" Annabelle cried, when she stood in front of a Rubens tangle of well-endowed female forms in various states of undress, being harried by robust gentlemen in capes and helmets.

"Notice the repetition of the curved forms, making an S-shaped pattern with the human bodies, drawing the eye around the composition. And the rich, nacreous hues of the flesh tones," Abbie said, pointing to a rotund naked haunch done in opalescent pinks and cream tones.

"No wonder they can't afford gowns," Kate said. "It would cost a fortune to cover all those pounds of flesh."

Not even the sublime Rembrandt portrait of a woman looking over a half door was spared their insightful criticism. "One would think the model could have taken off her apron and brushed her hair before having her portrait done," Annabelle tsk'd.

"Lovely curls. Soft," Mr. Singleton murmured, referring, of course, to his beloved. He clung like a barnacle to Annabelle throughout the tour.

The ninety minutes of the lesson seemed very long to them all, not least to their instructor. It was a great relief when Lord John appeared in the doorway.

Kate immediately escaped the tour and went running off to drag him forward. "Did you learn anything at the circus?" she asked.

His glinting smile revealed that he had. "I took a close look at O'Leary's wagon. You can see the traces of the name Brannigan under the yellow paint. It did not quite cover the darker blue beneath. I showed Algie. I wager he is having it out with O'Leary this minute. He was looking for O'Leary when he left the dancer. He was likely turning her up sweet with some trinket, as Mama suggested."

"I trust he did not give her any of the entailed jewelry," Lady Susan said.

"Egad, no. Algie is no flat. He would never part with the good jewelry, and as his pockets are to let at the moment, he could not buy her anything valuable. A box of bonbons or a pretty scarf is more like it."

Abbie made a mental note of all this. It confirmed her wretched opinion of Lord Penfel, and added an interesting point. His pockets were to let.

Lord John suggested a ride to pass the time until dinner. Kate and Lady Susan agreed. As there were only two ladies' mounts in the stable, it was arranged that Mr. Singleton would take Annabelle for a hurl in John's curricle.

Singleton braced himself to arrange it with Abbie. "Perfectly safe," he gasped. "Would not harm a hair of her head."

"Have no fear," Lord John added. "Singleton is a bang-up fiddler."

As his shyness made it unlikely he would be any sort of romantic menace, Abbie allowed the ride, so long as they were back within the hour. She went abovestairs with the girls while Kate and Lady Susan changed into their riding habits and Annabelle got her bonnet and pelisse. It was a relief to be rid of the unruly youngsters.

Abbie decided to continue her work on the Chardin and went below with her brushes, paints, canvas, and easel. She met Penfel at the bottom of the stairs as she descended.

"You should have rung for a footman," he said, taking the easel to carry for her.

It was not until they were in the gallery that it occurred to Abbie she was once again in an isolated place with Penfel. As he was helping her and generally behaving very well, she did not mention it. She felt she had trimmed him into line. He set her equipment up in front of the Chardin and brought her a chair.

"This is the picture O'Leary offered to sell for you?" he asked, studying her work.

"Yes, he has great faith in my talent, for as you can see, it's far from finished."

"But what is done is well-done," he said, cocking his head to study it from various angles. "Yes, I think you might give Chardin a run for his money. But why copy? Why not paint one of the girls?"

"One copies to discipline her hand. I do paint from the live model as well, of course. As to painting one of the girls, I would as lief try to paint a squirrel. They cannot sit still for a minute. Actually, I have a model in mind, but I doubt the one I want to paint would allow it."

Penfel wore a little smile of satisfaction. "Why do you not ask him?"

"Him? I was referring to Lady Penfel. I like to paint faces that have character. Older faces!" she added, when he looked offended.

"The milk is out of the bottle now, miss! Lack of character indeed. Is that really your assessment of me? I meant no harm this morning, truly. It is just that you looked so—"

"I was not referring to any moral deficiency, milord," she said hastily, "but to those lines and pouches that only come with age, and add expression to the physiognomy." She wondered how she had looked, that had urged him to kiss her.

"Is there no expression on this phiz, Miss Fairchild?" he demanded, pushing his finger into his chin for emphasis.

"Indeed there is," she replied, using the question as an excuse to study him. How bright his eyes were! And that strong chin. She would like to paint him outdoors, perhaps mounted on a horse, like a hero. When she realized her lips were curving in a smile, she drew herself back to business. "But do you really want that childish petulance put on canvas for posterity?" she asked.

"Shrew!" he said, smiling an intimate smile that robbed the word of offense.

"Spoiled brat," she replied blandly, and picked up her brush.

"Spoiled! Well, upon my word, that's pretty rich! I have had to scramble to keep Penfel together after—" He came to a sudden halt. "But Mama has washed enough dirty linen in public already. My hardships are not likely to impress a young lady who has to work for her living in any case."

She looked at him with interest. "Is that why your mama has such a strong dislike for your late papa? Did he cripple the estate?"

"He mortgaged anything that could be mortgaged. He was not a bad man, really. Not a womanizer or drinker or gambler, except upon 'Change, where he invariably lost. When he wanted to sell this collection," he said, waving his hand around the walls, "Mama threatened to take him to law, for it is entailed. They did not get along. He married her for her dowry; she married him because her papa made her. She was in love with some other fellow at the time. I think her anger is as much against her papa as her husband. Now that she has outlived them both, she is determined to enjoy her last years. And I encourage her to do so. She has earned it. It's appalling to think of being shackled for life to someone one does not respect or even like, say nothing of love. I am all for love matches. And after five years, I am now in a position not to have to marry for anything else. My affairs are in order."

The playful Penfel sounded sincere, and while Abbie was not quite ready to acquit him of his amorous attack on herself, she found this sufficient excuse for his behavior with the dancer. He was assuaging his heartbreak in the time-honored manner. "I am sorry Lady Eleanor did not accept your offer," she said.

A conscious look seized his mobile features. "Oh, as to that, I shall get over it."

"As you mean to marry for love, then one assumes you were in love with her. But I commend your common sense in determining to get over it. You should not let your heartbreak lead you amok. I am referring to your acquaintance with O'Leary," she added, lest he think she was harping on more personal peccadilloes.

"I only let O'Leary use the meadow to give the locals a little entertainment."

"You have made a friend of him, I think? A gentleman is known by the company he keeps. Perhaps a cardsharp and possible thief is not the optimum companion for the Earl of Penfel and Baron Rutcliffe and quasi-Lord Worley."

"Or even for Algernon Hatfield. That is who I am when I am not busy being a plurality of grand lords. Titles are no guarantee of character. Always excepting Marlborough and Wellington and a few others, I can think of few noblemen who attained their honors on merit. A tumble in the royal bedchamber is where most of us got our handles, that or some chicanery at court. Both, in the case of the Penfel honors."

He pointed to a portrait of a lady in a tiara, rubies, and the farthingale style of the seventeenth century, and said, "That is the lady who achieved nobility for herself and her family by a brief fling with Charles II. She was an actress, and she isn't even pretty, do you think?"

"No, not very," Abbie agreed. "The nose is somewhat pug, and the eyes too small for beauty."

"She was to Charles's taste, apparently, though he did not confer a dukedom on her husband, as he did on several of his bastards. I have little enough respect for titles. I would prefer you call me Algernon. And you, I think, are Abigail? Do your friends call you Abbie?"

"Certainly, when they have known me for a suitable length of time."

"What is a suitable length of time?"

His flirtatious manner warned her it was time for caution. "Three months," she said.

"That is somewhat arbitrary, *n'est-ce pas*? Surely, there are extenuating circumstances? Three months of occasional teas and assemblies would amount to— say, three hours a week. That is less than forty hours of actual familiarity. We, on the other hand, have shared a roof for—" He drew out his watch and glanced at it. "It is four o'clock. Going on thirty hours. At two o'clock tomorrow morning, you may call me Algie. In the unlikely case that I am in your company in the middle of the night, that is to say."

She refused to acknowledge his quizzing grin. "We have been in each other's company for only a few of those thirty hours you speak of, Lord Penfel."

"Have you never learned the arithmetic of romance, Miss Fairchild? Minutes count as hours when lovers are apart. Hours are but seconds when together." He came to a conscious stop. "I am cutting the ground out from under my own feet, am I not? It is that sly grin you are trying to conceal that distracted me. You are about to tell me we have only been together for seconds by that way of reckoning."

"Not at all. You were speaking of lovers. We are

98

not lovers. When a lady is with a congenital idiot, the seconds are hours. We are old friends by now."

"Excellent! Then, I shall call you Abbie."

"Oh—that is not what I meant!"

"What distracted *you*, I wonder?" he murmured.

"What would the young ladies think to hear you call me Abbie?"

"They would think us no better than we should be. One must always keep in mind the youngsters. I shall only call you Abbie on those too rare occasions when we are alone together—with a door open, of course." He inclined his head toward her and said in a conspiratorial tone, "Don't you adore secrets?"

"No, I save worship for church." Then she peered up and added, "But I like secrets," lest he take her for a confirmed prig.

His little chuckle was triumphant. "I knew there was a real woman lurking under that blue straitjacket!"

"And, one hopes, a real gentleman under that handsome Bath superfine jacket you wear with such élan."

He bowed. "My jacket and I thank you for the compliment. Our first, if I am not mistaken. I shall forever cherish this jacket."

She just shook her head at his nonsense. "About the key for the cartoons—"

"I see what you are about, miss. Butter the congenital idiot up, then wind him 'round your finger to have your way with him."

"You did promise."

"So I did, and before I earn a reprimand, I had best deliver. Come to my study when you are finished." He stopped, waiting for an objection to the venue chosen. When she didn't say anything, he continued, "You won't want to interrupt your work

99

here. There is no need to haul all your equipment back upstairs. Just leave it where it is. It is nice to see someone actually appreciating the collection."

"Thank you, Lord Penfel. You have no idea what it means to me."

He gazed at her face, rapt with delight, and said, "I think I do—Abbie."

Then he turned and left, smiling, and Abbie finally began to work on her Chardin. It was not until he was gone that she recalled they had not discussed that O'Leary and Brannigan were one and the same man. He had not said a word about that. Nor had she asked him about the journal he said O'Leary had carried, though she was certain he had not. It was difficult to concentrate on her work with these questions gnawing at her. After half an hour, she put it away and went to his study. She did not intend to actually go in, but just ask him for the key and leave.

The door stood open. A tea tray sat on the corner of the desk, suggesting that he would soon be back. She stood a moment at the door, looking up and down the hall, then stepped into the study to await him. She noticed the teacup was half full. When she touched the pot, it was still hot, so presumably he had just stepped out for a moment.

She glanced at the desk, admiring the chased silver ink pot and matching tray that held an assortment of pens. He had been writing a letter. It sat on the desk, the page half full. She averted her eyes, and noticed a ring sitting by the letter, partially covered by it. Curious, she looked at it again, without touching it. It was a lady's ring, gold with a large green stone.

Her breath suddenly caught in her throat. An emerald ring. The emerald ring stolen from Lady

Peevey! Yes, it was certainly the same one. A baguette stone, edged all around with diamonds, as described in the journal. Her hand flew to her lips to stifle the gasp of astonishment. What was it doing here?

Black thoughts whirled in her mind like bats in a small room. Penfel had been at Peevey's house. O'Leary had been nearby. They were friends. Penfel had certainly lied about O'Leary showing him that article in the journal, and now Penfel had this stolen ring. He must have lost heavily to O'Leary at cards. If he was in the man's debt, he could be made to dance to his tune—even to the extent of having his own treasures plundered. He had said himself they were insured.

It was hard to come to any but the logical conclusion. Penfel was O'Leary's cohort. He was a thief, and a scoundrel. Had Lady Eleanor or Lord Peevey become suspicious? Was that why he had been turned off? Had he ever even loved Lady Eleanor? He spoke of marrying for love, yet he was remarkably blasé at her refusing his offer. Had Lady Eleanor been only an excuse to spy out the secrets of Peevey Castle?

She turned and darted up to her bedchamber and closed the door to contemplate what she had just discovered, and more importantly, what she should and could do about it.

Chapter Eleven

As Abbie paced to and fro in her chamber, she tried to make sense of this enigma called Lord Penfel. She remembered various conversations with him and about him. He had boasted he had his financial affairs in order, yet Lord John said his brother's pockets were to let. O'Leary's offering Penfel a chance to win back the blunt he had lost at cards suggested gambling was his weakness. That and, of course, women. His own mama had accused him of being too fond of women. Lady Susan, on the other hand, had said he was not a lecher, and Lady Susan knew everything, or gave that impression.

She thought of their recent conversation in the gallery, when he had seemed completely carefree, flirting, happy. And all the while that stolen ring sat in his office, or in his pocket. Did he have no conscience at all, or was it possible she was misreading the evidence, that he was innocent? He might have won the ring from O'Leary in a card game. But O'Leary would not wager such an incriminating thing. Penfel knew the ring was stolen, so that excuse would not do. Excuse? Why was she looking for an excuse for him? He was nothing to her. She scarcely knew the man.

She only knew her heart beat faster when she was

with him, that his smile made her feel special, that when she was in this house, her eyes were always on the door when he was not present, and on him when he was. She knew that, while she had acted grossly offended at his embrace, her heart had thrilled to it. She told herself it was only infatuation, and she was fortunate to have found out his true character before infatuation deepened to love, and tried to believe it.

Very well then, accept that Penfel was a man of weak character. What should she do? She could report him to Bow Street, but they would be intimidated by a noble criminal and palmed off with some explanation. Nothing would result but embarrassment and ill feelings all around. The kinder and more sensible thing would be to confront Penfel face-to-face, and get a promise from him to return his ill-got gains and sever his connection with O'Leary. And if he refused, then she would resort to Bow Street. At least he would be forced to stop stealing if he knew Bow Street was watching him. And he would hate her forever.

She steeled herself for the coming confrontation and returned to Penfel's study. The door was closed. When she knocked, no one answered, and when she tried the handle, the door was locked. She went in search of Sifton, who told her Penfel had decided to ride out and join Lord John and the ladies. He had forgotten all about her. He was supposed to give her the key to the Leonardo cartoons.

"Did he leave a key for me?" she inquired.

"No, ma'am. He didn't. Perhaps I can help?"

"It was the key for the da Vinci cartoons."

"Oh, I am afraid I do not have that key, ma'am. His lordship has it. Shall I remind him when he returns?"

"Never mind. I shall do it myself, if you would notify me when he comes back."

"Certainly, madam."

She returned abovestairs and worried for another half hour until the girls came back. Kate told her that Penfel had not joined them, but she had seen him talking to a man on the road half a mile from Penfel Hall.

"O'Leary?" Abbie asked, her stomach churning.

"No, Miss Fairchild. We did meet *him*. I was going to tell you. Susan stopped a moment to talk, but I rode back to hear what she was saying, and it was nothing of any importance."

"What was it?"

"Just something about Lord Sylvester. O'Leary thought he had met him."

This sounded fairly harmless. "What about the man Penfel met?"

"He was just a little ordinary-looking man. Not a gentleman. He looked like a racetrack tout."

"I see."

That Penfel had lied to Sifton told her he was ashamed to admit who he was really meeting. It sounded like another colleague of O'Leary's. Perhaps a fence Penfel was selling the emerald ring to, as his pockets were to let.

"Why are you so curious about Penfel? Did you have a rendezvous with him?" Kate asked, and did not wait for an answer. "He is terribly handsome, quite like John. Don't you love being in love, Miss Fairchild? How Slats would stare if we came back engaged ladies."

"Don't be so foolish," Abbie scoffed, and turned away to hide her blush.

Dinnertime was fast approaching, and Spadger

was bustling about to assist the young ladies with their evening toilettes. Abbie took care of her own dressing. In a dispirited mood, she wore a navy gown and took no particular care for her coiffure. The pale face and haunted eyes staring back at her from her mirror made her look like a ghost. She pinched her cheeks and bit her lips to give her some color, but when she essayed a smile, it was a sad travesty.

This visit that had begun so pleasantly was fast turning into a nightmare. From their first meeting, Penfel had seemed to fancy her. Her first idea that he only did it to discourage Lady Susan could not account for all his attentions to herself. Most of them occurred when Susan was nowhere near them. Was he just one of those gentlemen who always flirted with any decent-looking female who crossed his path? At least he did not badger the young girls, say that for him.

Spadger came dashing into Abbie's room for one of her private words after she had attended to the young ladies.

"I believe Lady Susan is up to something, Miss Fairchild."

This was no real cause for alarm. Spadger always made a mountain of a molehill. "What is it, Spadger?"

"I saw her take a *billet doux* out of her reticule. She looked at it and smiled. You don't suppose that beast of an O'Leary has got at her?"

"Are you sure it was a *billet doux*?"

"It was a piece of paper. What else could it be but a letter?"

"She had a letter from her mama this morning."

"Ah, well, that could be it, then."

Abbie could not believe Susan was carrying on a

105

clandestine correspondence with O'Leary. It was not her style.

At seven o'clock, the butler had still not notified Abbie of Penfel's return. When she took the girls belowstairs, he beckoned her aside and said, "His lordship just came in, madam. As he was in a hurry to change for dinner, I did not bother notifying you. I knew you would see him when he came downstairs."

"Thank you, Sifton."

Penfel had apparently hurried his toilette, for he joined them within minutes. Crook or not, Abbie acknowledged that he looked devastatingly handsome in a close-fitting bottle-green jacket, with a small emerald in his cravat. She had never seen such a dashing smile as he turned on her the moment he entered the room. It lingered on her for a long moment, softening as he gazed into her eyes, and seemed to say a hundred intimate things that could not be said aloud in company. It was almost a caress. When she realized she was gazing back at him in the same moonling sort of way, she lowered her head and fiddled with her fan.

The younger members of the party made lively conversation during the interval before dinner when a glass of sherry was served. The young ladies were allowed a glass of wine. They had to learn how to handle it before their debut. Abbie watched Susan for signs of discomposure or excitement, but found she behaved as usual. She was explaining to Kate why her mount had stumbled at the fence.

"You pulled in when you should have given him his head."

"I did not! I hate horses that refuse a jump."

"Mr. Singleton is going to let me take the reins tomorrow," Annabelle said.

"Is he, by God!" Lord John cried. "If Miss Kirby lames my nags, you will pay the price, Singleton."

Singleton blushed and made a demurring murmur.

Abbie was grateful for their high spirits. It helped conceal the silence of her own dismal mood. When Penfel, after a few words with his mama, came and sat beside her, she could think of nothing to say. What they had to discuss could not be said in public.

"I waited fifteen hours for you to come for the key," he said. "That is fifteen hours by romance time. I made sure you would not be five minutes after me. Is it possible da Vinci is losing his appeal?" The questioning uncertainty of his look implied it was his own appeal that concerned him. "I even ordered tea. Why didn't you come to my study? Was it the location that kept you away?"

"I went later. You weren't there," she said distractedly. She wondered if the emerald ring was in his pocket even now, or if it was already on its way to London with the man who looked like a race tout.

"I received a note and had to go out to meet a friend."

That would be the man Kate had seen him talking to. Obviously, no real friend but a business acquaintance. Penfel was not an accomplished liar. He had told Sifton he was going to meet Lord John and the girls.

"You might have left the key with the butler," she said.

"And missed seeing your face when you first beheld the da Vinci's? Not likely! I have been looking forward to that moment, Miss Fairchild. See how carefully I guard our secret?" He looked, waiting for some bantering reply. When she just looked at him

107

sadly, he said in a voice suddenly serious, "What is the matter?"

"Could I have a word with you in private after dinner?"

Her request seemed to please him, to judge by his smile. "Strange you should say that. I was about to suggest the same thing. Our minds are beginning to become attuned. By the by, I spoke to Mama. She would be flattered to death to have her portrait taken. She is not happy with the Reynolds portrait done when she was young. I have not had my own portrait painted yet. Perhaps I have found the artist to do it, if you could lower yourself to paint a phiz with no character."

This casual remark, that would have thrilled her to death yesterday, was only another hammer blow to her spirits, to think of losing such a marvelous opportunity. She would never be allowed to do either portrait once he realized she knew he was a thief.

Lady Penfel's ears perked up at hearing her name spoken. "What is that you say, Algie? Are you talking about my picture? Reynolds made me look like a nun, all in white with the gown cut up to my chin. I plan to wear a red feather in my hair and a low-cut purple gown to show my new freedom when Miss Fairly paints me. They will never show it at Somerset House, but when I am gone, I want my descendants to know what I was really like. But you must take it easy on my wrinkles and crow's-feet. Algie says you like wrinkles. What do you think of my idea, Miss Fairmont?"

"I think you would look charming, with or without wrinkles, ma'am. I only hope I am up to the challenge of portraying your vivacity."

"Vivacity! I like that! Ha, she is a cozener, like

108

you, Algie. You are right, I am beginning to like this chit. You are softening up her schoolmistressy ways. We will have her laughing and dancing and wearing red shoes in no time."

Abbie felt a flush warm her cheeks to learn that Penfel had been discussing her with his mama. She felt sure he did not discuss all his women so freely. She meant more to him than the dancer at least. But it was the dancer who would be with him at two o'clock in the morning, when they were to have reached the intimacy of a first-name basis.

The conversation continued lively over a dinner of two courses and two removes. Abbie noticed that the meal was noticeably grander than last night, and wondered at the improvement. She enjoyed it less, however, even though she was seated at Penfel's left side. She did not mention this new seating arrangement, nor did he, but he gave her a speaking look when he motioned her to his side and drew her chair. He tried to engage her in flirtation a few times over the turbot, once over the fowl and later over the veal collops, but she was unable to respond.

It was not until the chantilly and almond paste tarts were served that he leaned toward her and said in a low voice, "Is it the menu that displeases you, when I have harried Cook to do her best, or have you taken a vow of silence, Miss Fairchild? You are as quiet as Singleton this evening."

"I was thinking about something," she said.

"The red feather and purple gown will be a sad trial to be sure." He studied her a moment, and when she did not reply, he said, "What is really bothering you, my dear?"

She felt tears sting her eyes at that tender "my dear" that had slipped out, unnoticed, she thought.

"We shall talk later," she said, blinking away the tears.

"The port will get short shrift this evening. Shall we say, eight-thirty, in my study? I want no misunderstandings this time, as we stumbled into this afternoon. I promise you shall get the key—that will ensure your coming. You see how easy it is when you have put the lord of the manor in good spirits?"

"What happens when he ceases to smile on me?" she asked, with a mental sigh to think that all this adventure would soon be over.

"I am gratified that the thought of that day appalls you—to judge by those sad eyes. Let us hope it does not occur any time soon, say for the next eighty or ninety years."

"Is that romance time, or Greenwich time?"

"Oh, good! You're getting over your little fit of pique."

Lady Penfel observed her son's enchantment and called down the table, "Up to your old flirting ways, Algie? I hope you are not misleading Miss Fairway into taking you too seriously?"

"I find the young ladies nowadays uncommonly well able to look after themselves, Mama."

"You are right, of course. Tough as boiled owls, as they need to be in this man's world."

Lady Susan apparently heard only a part of the conversation. She looked up and said, "Was that a boiled owl we were eating earlier, ma'am? I made sure it was a goose that had not hung long enough."

Lady Penfel's "Gudgeon!" was audible the length of the table. "No, it was an owl," she replied mischievously.

"Do owls make you wiser, like eating fish?" Annabelle asked. "Because of the saying, 'wise old owl,' you know."

Lady Penfel said, "Yes, they do. Pity Miss Slatkin does not serve you gels more owl."

"I would hate owl!" Kate said. "Oh, you are funning, milady! Is your mama not funning, Lord John?"

"Of course she is. The fowl was a buzzard."

The conversation deteriorated into foolishness, and Abbie ate her chantilly without tasting it. Her qualms about conversing with the nobility had been unnecessary. Their conversation was not more elevated than her uncle's monologues about Mysore, but it was a deal livelier. She would have enjoyed it, were it not for the worries that lay like a dark pall over her heart.

Chapter Twelve

The gentlemen's taking of port was brief that evening, but it seemed a long time to the anxiously waiting Miss Fairchild. One matter of interest occurred in the interim. While the girls chattered about beaux and balls, Lady Penfel beckoned Abbie to her side.

"I have just had an inspiration, Miss Fairview," she said. "I want to be painted as Cleopatra." Abbie blinked in confusion. "That is the sort of creature I should like to have been. I see you goggle at the thought of painting a hag like myself as Cleopatra, but you misunderstand my meaning. In the Manuscript Room we have an etching of Cleopatra done by some French fellow—I cannot recall the name— but she is sitting on a stone bench in front of a tent, with a lion at her feet. It is called *After Actium*. That is the battle she and Mark Antony lost, you know, when her inevitable end was in sight. A moment of utter desperation one would think, but it does not kill her spirit. She is still noble and proud, even in defeat. Her chin is up, she gazes into the distance with a queenly gaze, uncaring that life has bested her.

"It is that pose, that expression I want on my face, not her strange coiffure and outfit. That straight hair would never suit me. I shall title it *After Penfel*, referring to Bruce and Penfel Hall, for when Algie marries, I shall leave Penfel Hall. It is how we ladies are treated—kicked out of our homes after giving life service to our husbands, their families, and their estates."

"I cannot think Lord Penfel would force you out of your home, ma'am!"

"Of course he would not! This is not about Algie. It is about me, about us ladies not having any rights. If Algie and Johnnie were to die, God forbid, my daughters would not inherit Penfel. It would go to some wretched cousin in Cornwall, only because he wears trousers. It is a trick the gentlemen have rigged up to keep things to themselves. They call it primogeniture. I call it common thievery. Come, I'll show you the etching. I wonder how I came to think of it. I daresay it was that little smirk you all wore when we discussed red feathers and a purple gown."

"We shall have to get the key from Lord Penfel," Abbie said. Her mind flew to the da Vinci cartoons. She remembered Penfel saying he wanted to see her face when she first beheld them. Now it seemed Lady Penfel might be the one to see her face, because she knew that if the cartoons were there, she could not await the tardy Penfel's pleasure to view them.

"We don't need a key. The Manuscript Room is never locked. We only use it for storing family records and a few rubbishing old pictures not good enough to hang on the walls."

One could hardly call the da Vinci drawings rubbishing old pictures. Abbie had already decided her hostess was perilously close to the edge of lunacy,

113

and assumed she didn't know the room was locked. The butler had confirmed that it was, and that Penfel had the only key. Lady Penfel rose, urging "Miss Fairway" to follow her. In her various talks with Penfel, Abbie had never learned exactly where in the vast house the Manuscript Room was located. She was led down a long corridor, around a corner to a chamber across from the library. The oak-paneled door opened with a simple twist of the knob.

"Grab a candelabra," the dame said, and Abbie took a heavy branched candelabra from a table in the hallway.

They went into a long, narrow, dark chamber, a sort of second, smaller library with a worktable in the center of the room, but with closed cabinets instead of bookshelves lining the walls. While Abbie lit a few lamps, Lady Penfel began rooting through the cabinets.

"Where are the da Vinci cartoons kept?" Abbie asked.

"I am trying to remember. The French etchings are in one of these cupboards." She slammed a door and opened another. "Here we are! These are the French pictures," she cried, and drew out a dusty leather folio. Abbie was appalled that the priceless cartoons were kept in such a careless manner, vulnerable to dust, damp, and mice.

"It is right here on top," Lady Penfel said, lifting up an aging parchment and placing it on the table. "I have not seen it in years, but it is just as I remember. I was fond of this picture. I daresay I identified with Cleopatra's indomitable spirit even in those days, though I didn't realize what ailed me. Too distracted with having babies—all those girls, and they are not

114

the consolation one hears they are, either. At least mine aren't. They married and moved far away. I seldom see them since I have quit doing the Season."

The etching was as she had described it. Cleopatra's expression was grave, but not defeated. In the background, the ruins of her army stood in disarray. Bodies lay on the ground, spears and helmets abandoned in the dust.

"I shall sit on that stone bench in the garden, with Penfel Hall in the background," Lady Penfel said. "Pity I do not have a lion, but I daresay a large dog will do as well, eh? Cuddles will rest at my feet."

"Yes. Will you still wear the red feather and purple gown?"

"No, I think for this sort of picture, I want to look pathetic. I shall wear a very simple chemise, perhaps ragged 'round the hem, and bare feet. Cook will have something suitable." She set the etching aside. "We shall take this along with us."

"Are the da Vinci cartoons there?" Abbie asked, as Lady Penfel closed the folio and took it back to the cupboard.

"They are somewhere amid this rubble," the dame said. "You can come back later and have a root about for them, if you like. I daresay we should return to the saloon now. Otherwise, Lady Susan will read me a lecture. You don't think Algie will offer for her?" She took the Cleopatra etching, Abbie blew out the candles, and they left.

"I shouldn't think so, ma'am. I have not noticed any closeness between them."

"No, I shouldn't think he could stomach her, even if she has twenty-five thousand. I daresay that is why her mama wanted me to ask her here. Nettie cannot have heard about Lady Eleanor. As soon as ever I clamped an eye on Susan, I knew it was hopeless. She has not improved one iota from her last visit five years ago. Miss Fenshaw is more like it. She has no conversation worth the name, but she is a lively little thing. It seems she has a sweet tooth for our Johnnie, though. What is her dot?"

"Twenty thousand, I believe."

"Not bad for a younger son."

When they returned to the saloon, Lord John and Singleton had joined the ladies. Abbie was surprised Penfel was not there, as he had told her he would curtail the taking of port. Singleton noticed her surprise and girded himself to choke out a few words. "Penfel—tell you—study."

"Thank you," Abbie said, filling in the gaps and assuming Penfel had asked Singleton to relay the message.

She headed to the study. As she went along the corridor, she wrestled with the coming visit. There was no point beating about the bush, and giving him time to invent some story, or divert her with lovemaking. She would just come right out with it. His door was closed when she got there. She gave a sharp rap and stepped in, knowing he was awaiting her. He sat at his desk, facing her. He rose and smiled as she entered—a rather nervous, edgy smile, not the usual warm greeting.

"Lord Penfel, I know all about your relationship with O'Leary," she said.

His face stiffened to ice. "I have never concealed that O'Leary and I are friends."

"And business colleagues, I think?"

He stepped out from behind the desk, looking as if he meant to eject her. She stepped back. "This

116

has nothing to do with you!" he said in a cold voice she had never heard before. "I am busy at the moment, Miss Fairchild. Perhaps you could come back later."

"Busy planning more thefts? I know you and he are robbing houses. I saw the emerald ring on your desk this afternoon, the one that was stolen from Lady Peevey recently, when you were at Lewes, so pray do not try to fob me off with some Banbury tale."

She could hardly be unaware of Penfel's fury. His eyes blazed like hot coals. As she rushed on with her charges, she noticed something else as well. Penfel's glares at her were alternated with sharp glances over her shoulder. She looked, and saw O'Leary, regarding her through narrowed eyes. He was partially concealed by the open door. He must have been on his way out when she barged in, and got caught behind the door. If she had not been so upset, she would have seen him.

"You are acquainted with Mr. O'Leary, I think?" Penfel said.

Her first reaction was a dreadful embarrassment, to see O'Leary there, listening to her accusations. She had to remind herself what she had said was true, that he and Penfel were the ones who should be embarrassed. She lifted her chin and turned to stare at Penfel.

"Scheming to commit more robberies, milord?" she asked.

"You misunderstand the matter," Penfel said in a glacial voice. "You had best run along. As you can see, my friend and I are busy. I shall speak to you about this misunderstanding later."

O'Leary stepped forward, wearing an ingratiating

smile. "About that ring, my dear, I won it in a card game in Lewes. If the fellow I won it from stole it, that is not my fault." He hesitated a moment, then added, "Lord Penfel won it from me the next night."

"Everyone knows you are Brannigan, Mr. O'Leary," she said. "You ought to have given your wagon two coats of paint. The former name shows through the yellow." She turned to Penfel. "Surely, Lord John told you!"

Penfel and O'Leary exchanged a brief but meaningful glance. Conspiratorial was the word that occurred to Abbie. Even menacing.

"I bought the wagon off Brannigan!" O'Leary said at once. "He had to sell up when things got too hot for him. You believe me, Penfel?"

"Of course," Penfel said.

Then he came forward and took Abbie by the elbow to lead her to the door, opened it, and shoved her out. "Later!" he growled, under his breath.

She went, trembling, back to the saloon to await him. The room was empty, the lamps turned low. Light glinted from the gilt picture frames, and some brass bibelots. She sat, thinking about that wretched confrontation. It had not gone as she hoped. O'Leary's presence made everything more difficult. She had hoped to try to convince Penfel to change his errant ways. But he had obviously no intention of changing. He had chosen O'Leary over her, over common decency, over doing the right thing.

Sifton came in, peering through the shadows, and began to turn up the lamps.

"Her ladyship and the gentlemen have taken the ladies to the circus, Miss Fairchild," he said. "I could ask a footman to take you along to join them, if you

118

wish. Her ladyship thought you wished to study some etchings in the Manuscript Room this evening."

"You told me the Manuscript Room was kept locked, Sifton, that you did not have the key," she said.

He looked offended. "There must have been some misunderstanding, ma'am. I thought it was the da Vinci cartoons you wished to see. His lordship keeps them under lock and key. The Manuscript Room is always open."

"It is the da Vincis I wish to see."

She was still talking to the butler when hurrying footsteps sounded in the hallway. The butler went out to investigate. From the open doorway, Abbie saw O'Leary heading toward the front door. The butler handed him his hat, cane, and gloves, and he left. Before the door had closed, another patter of footfalls sounded, and Penfel appeared. He peered into the saloon. When he saw Abbie, he stopped and strode in, stiff-legged. His eyes were still blazing with anger, his face a mask of fury.

"May I speak to you for a moment in my study, Miss Fairchild?" he said in a voice that made refusal pointless.

She answered his fury with a fiery eye and a sneering, "I have been looking forward to it, milord."

Penfel said something in a quiet aside to the butler, who nodded his acquiescence. Then Penfel led Abbie down the corridor to his study. When they reached the doorway, she halted, suddenly frightened. What had he said to Sifton? Was it an order to turn a deaf ear to any appeals for help? If Penfel was a thief, to what lengths would he go to conceal it? Was her very life in danger? Her fear began to rise to panic. Should she call for help, should she bolt?

As she stood, undecided, he reached out, clamped a strong hand around her wrist, and dragged her into his study. Then he slammed the door and turned on her in wrathful fury.

Chapter Thirteen

"What in hell's name do you think you're doing?" Penfel demanded. His angry voice rolled like thunder in the closed room. The obsidian glint in his dark eyes was a flash of lightning. When she noticed his hands were bunched into fists, Abbie suddenly felt her knees turn to water. She swallowed the lump of fear in her throat and took a step backward. Yet she knew that flight wasn't the solution.

She took a deep breath and said in a tremulous voice that was trying to sound brave, "I should warn you, milord, I have already notified Bow Street what is going forth here. If anything should happen to me, they will know where to lay the blame."

"Are you mad!" he cried. "Two months work gone down the drain."

"It will be your whole life if you get caught! Why in God's name can you not just marry an heiress like all the other bankrupt lords if you have ruined yourself with gambling?"

"Ruined? Did I not tell you this very day I have brought Penfel around?"

"Then, why have you hooked up with that wretch of an O'Leary to rob your friends? Who is next? Do you plan to rob Penfel Hall?"

"Rob myself? Your wits are gone begging, woman."

He turned and began to pace back and forth, raking his hands through his hair.

Abbie remained near the safety of the door, though her first fear had lessened. "You mentioned insurance, I believe," she said.

"So that is your opinion of me! That I am a common ken smasher."

"No, sir, a very uncommon one. I cannot recall any other noble gentleman sunk so low. And don't try to con me you won that emerald ring from O'Leary, for he would not dare to use it as a pawn if you were not in league with him. You knew very well it was stolen from Peevey."

"Of course I knew! I didn't win it from O'Leary."

"You have your henchmen well trained to defend you. No need to ask where you did get it."

"I got it from Sadie Hutchins, one of O'Leary's dancing girls. He's in love with her. He gave it to her for her birthday, but warned her not to wear it yet. She asked me if it were a real emerald. I managed to talk the ring out of her—without O'Leary's knowledge."

"This goes from bad to worse. Preying on helpless women!"

"Will you please wait until I have finished, before leaping to the wrong conclusions. Sadie asked me to take it to a jeweler to discover if the ring was genuine."

"After you convinced her it was not."

"Precisely. And, incidentally, like the rest of her species, she is about as helpless as a tiger shark."

"The last I heard, men and women were from the same species, milord. Homo sapiens. And what has this to do with you and O'Leary robbing houses?"

"Schoolmistress!" he grumbled. "Why do you think I let the scoundrel come here? Sit down," he said, still angry, but trying to gain control of his pounding heart.

Abbie sat, peering hopefully to discover how Penfel might be redeemed.

He dropped into the chair behind the desk, wiped his fingers over his chin and began. "The first I heard of O'Leary was six months ago, when he robbed Halford Hall, near Birmingham. He was calling himself Brannigan then. His circus had passed through town a few weeks before. He scouts out vulnerable homes while his circus is in the area, and comes back later to rob them. When the same thing happened to the Scotts' a month later, the Scotts noticed the connection to Brannigan. The third robbery pretty well confirmed it. But when Bow Street went after Brannigan, he had vanished.

"He laid low for a few months, then O'Leary's Circus suddenly appeared on the scene, working the border territory between Kent and Sussex, well removed from his first crimes, and the story began to repeat itself. When O'Leary moved on to Lewes, Ollie Wincham—that is Peevey's son, a friend of mine—asked me to help trap O'Leary. I visited Peevey on the pretext of dangling after Lady Eleanor." Abbie perked up her ears at this news. Penfel gazed directly into her eyes and said, "There was never anything between us. In fact, she is half engaged to Rawlins. My job was to pretend I was out at pocket, and strike up a friendship with O'Leary, but he revealed nothing. We were pretty sure it was Peevey's place that would be smashed, as indeed it was."

"How does it come you didn't catch O'Leary, if you knew his plans?"

Penfel scowled. "Because the man is a weasel. We

lay in wait for him after the circus had left. Every night we were on guard, pistols cocked. He didn't come. What he did was slip in at the library door in broad daylight one afternoon during Peevey's public day and lift what he found lying about downstairs. Fortunately, he didn't get upstairs to the safe. That is when I took the decision to let him use my meadow. O'Leary's next stop was to be Burgess Hill, not far from here. He had arranged to use the commons for his show. I had a word with the local authorities, and they told O'Leary there was opposition to the circus, the residents didn't want it. Then I 'accidentally' met O'Leary in a tavern one night. That is when I offered him the use of my land, pretending I needed the hundred pounds he paid me."

After mulling all this over for a moment, Abbie could find no inconsistency in the tale. "Were you not afraid he'd rob you?" she asked.

"I knew he would try. He's in the house every chance he gets, seeing what is worth taking, and how best to get at it. I told him I am off to London next week, to give him the impression he would have easy pickings here. And when he comes back this time, we'll be ready for him, day or night. Bow Street is watching him like a hawk." Penfel stopped, frowned, and sighed. "Not that he'll try anything now. The man is no fool. He'll disappear. O'Reilly's or Rooney's or McCoon's Circus will be born in some distant county, and it will start all over again."

"What of the things he steals? Can they not be traced back to him?"

"Eventually, perhaps. He farms them out to Stop Hole Abbey. Buyers of stolen goods at bargain prices are not likely to report where they got them."

"Well, you might have told me all this sooner!"

"I didn't want you involved. If Mama had told me she was inviting a parcel of schoolgirls here, I would have put the visit off. You were already here when I arrived. Short of sending you packing, what could I do?"

"I would be very happy to leave! Unfortunately, I cannot take the girls back to Miss Slatkin's. The school is closed for the week. Perhaps I could take them to my uncle's house in Maidstone. He is in London."

"It is not necessary now," Penfel said grimly. "O'Leary knows I know. How did you come to call on me, when I asked John to tell you not to come to my office?"

"Lord John said nothing to me. It was Singleton. He muttered something. I thought he was telling me to go to your study, as we had arranged earlier."

"I wish someone would teach that man to speak."

"What do you think O'Leary will do?" she asked.

"He'll have his revenge eventually. A few months from now, when I have forgotten all about it, I shall come home and find the silver gone and the gallery rifled. He'll watch his p's and q's for the present."

"I'm sorry," she said in a small voice. But her sorrow was mitigated by the knowledge that Penfel was not a criminal. She looked at him uncertainly, wondering how much of his anger was directed at her, and how much at O'Leary.

"It's not your fault," he admitted. "Did you really contact Farber? How the deuce did you know he was a Runner? It was supposed to be a secret."

"Farber? Oh, is that the man you met this afternoon when you let on you were going to meet a friend?"

"That's him. If you didn't know—But of course, you were following the villain. Me."

"I was not! I didn't think of it. It was Kate who saw you. She mentioned it to me. I only told you I had contacted Bow Street in case you—you meant to murder me," she said, and suddenly felt extremely foolish.

A reluctant smile tugged at his lips. "I shan't say I didn't feel like it. Damnation. I wonder what O'Leary will do now. He won't take this sitting down."

"What did he say after I left?"

"We played a game of charades. I pretended not to know what you were talking about, and he pretended to believe me. If your announcement that I knew he was Brannigan did not give it away, the emerald ring did. Fortunately, he didn't actually see it. After you left, I described it as a quite different sort of emerald ring to O'Leary. I ought to go see if Sadie is all right. He'll be furious that she let me take it. In fact, I'll give it back to her. If she can show it to him, he might believe that the ring you saw really was a different one." He studied Abbie a moment and added offhandedly, "By the by, the ring is the only thing I wanted or got from Sadie."

Something in the way he looked at her belied his offhanded manner and made her blush. "I told you, you don't have to explain to me," she said, feeling foolish as she had come to his office to demand an explanation.

Penfel didn't seem to notice the inconsistency, however. "Yes, I do," he said. "I don't want you to think me a lecher. A thief and a murderer are bad enough, but you have already informed me lechery tops the interdict list, where ladies are concerned.

126

What will you do while I am gone? Would you care to look at the cartoons?"

It seemed an unlikely moment for him to make this suggestion, when things were so confused. She soon figured out that he just wanted to keep her busy, so she would not further complicate his work.

"Where do you really keep them? I know they are not in the Manuscript Room. I have been there with your mama."

"I have them locked away. I'll show you."

"Later. I am not in the mood to appreciate them just now."

He nodded. "Don't leave the house, Abbie. O'Leary might decide to wreak some revenge on you."

"Could you not have Farber arrest him?"

"He could be arrested on suspicion, but his lawyer would soon have him out. We need evidence to get a conviction." He unlocked the top drawer of his desk and drew out the emerald ring.

"Is that not evidence?" she asked.

"Just one item is not enough. How could we prove he didn't win it in a card game, as he claims?"

As he spoke, there was a sharp rap at the door. Abbie's heart jumped into her throat. "O'Leary!" she whispered.

"Stay here," he said, and put the ring in his pocket. "There's a loaded pistol in that top right-hand drawer, if you should need it." He went to the door, opened it, and stepped into the hall.

Abbie, her heart thumping like a wild thing, went to the drawer and took out the pistol. It felt heavy, deadly. Surely, O'Leary would not try to kill Penfel in his own house? She tiptoed to the door and put her ear to it. The voice on the other side was not O'Leary's Irish lilt. It was a rough, common voice.

"Nary a sign of her," it said grimly.

Abbie opened the door and peeked out.

Penfel turned and stared at her with eyes that looked black. "Susan is gone," he said.

She stared in confusion. "What do you mean, gone? She went to the circus with your mama and the others."

"She isn't with them. They were all watching the show. It seems no one noticed her leaving. The youngsters went to buy lemonade. Everyone thought she was with someone else. John thought Susan was with Singleton and Miss Kirby, and vice versa. When they returned, they learned Mama thought she was with the youngsters. She has vanished. O'Leary is gone as well."

"Good God! Could Spadger be right?"

"Who is Spadger?" Penfel asked in confusion, as he had not met that good woman.

"She said Susan had a *billet doux*. I made sure it was only that letter from her mama."

"Susan would never go voluntarily to meet O'Leary," Penfel said at once. "She holds herself too high."

"She's been talking to him a few times, though."

Farber spoke up. "I figured O'Leary was accounted for as there were lamps burning in his wagon, but when one of the workers went and tapped at his door, there was no answer. I went in and looked about as soon as the man had left. O'Leary was gone—packed up his personal belongings and sneaked out the back way. My fear is that he's kidnapped Lady Susan."

Abbie read an accusation in the grim lines of Penfel's mouth and glinting eyes: "This is what your demmed interference has caused."

What he actually said, in a high, bewildered voice,

128

was "I'm ruined. A duke's daughter, under my protection, kidnapped from my house."

"It's not your fault, Penfel. I was in charge of her!" Abbie said.

Farber spoke again, with aplomb and assurance. "You can parcel out the blame later, folks. Whoever is at fault, we had best get busy and find her, before some harm befalls the poor girl."

Chapter Fourteen

While Lady Susan had displayed some interest in O'Leary, Abbie could not believe she would be involved in anything so déclassé as a runaway match with a fortune hunter, and she had pegged him as one from the start. Such folly was not her style. She would want a noble husband, with all the pomp and nobility and royalty the duke could summon to attend her nuptials. If she was with O'Leary, she was there under duress, and she must be rescued at once.

Abovestairs, Spadger assured Abbie that Lady Susan had not returned to her room. Her clothing and personal items were all there, as she had left them. Her pearls with the diamond pendant were in her jewelry box. Of the letter, possibly a *billet doux*, there was no sign.

Servants were sent scrambling through the house to make sure she was not in the library, the morning parlor, or any of the small parlors. Footmen searched the grounds and stable, to determine that no horses or carriages were missing. When Abbie returned belowstairs, Sifton told her his lordship and Farber had gone to the circus grounds.

"I shall join them," she said, and darted above-stairs for her bonnet and pelisse.

A footman was waiting with the butler in the entrance hall when she returned.

"Before he left, his lordship informed me Quilp was to accompany you if you *insisted* on going, ma'am," Sifton said. She ignored his disapproving face and the derogatory emphasis on "insisted."

Quilp was a senior footman, a sensible fellow of forty odd years. Protocol was forgotten during this moment of crisis. Abbie fretted openly about the missing girl as they hastened through the darkness to the meadow, and Quilp replied as if to an equal.

"Her ladyship don't seem the sort for any freakish start. Stands very high on her dignity at all times. There's not much goes up to her chamber that don't come back down for being too cold or too hot or not to her liking in some way. She gave Mary, the downstairs maid, a rare Bear Garden jaw for not seeing her gloves were taken up to her room when she left them on the table in the hall. Seems it's not how things are done at Wycliffe. Or even at Elmgrove." Then he recalled his lowly position and added perfunctorily, "A very fine lady."

They met up with the party from the Hall at the fairgrounds. Penfel and Farber were with them. Lady Penfel had convinced herself that Lady Susan had felt unwell and gone back to the Hall. Penfel had just told them she was missing, and the girls were all in a flutter.

"Whatever will Slats say!" Annabelle worried.

"Never mind Slats. What will her papa, the duke say!" Kate exclaimed, her eyes as big as saucers.

Lady Penfel frowned. "It is not like Susan to do anything raffish. I fear that rogue has got her. Such a nuisance. Nettie will be very put out with us. You must get busy and find her, Algie. Tonight—or one

131

of you boys will have to marry her. We cannot return her to Wycliffe a ruined lady, or we would never hear the end of it."

Strangely, none of Lady Susan's best friends expressed much concern for her safety, but only for what others would say.

During the melee, Kate Fenshaw sidled up to Abbie and whispered, "Do you think it possible Susan arranged it herself, Miss Fairchild?"

"Did she seem very fond of O'Leary?"

"Oh, no. That was not my meaning. I meant did she do it to force Penfel's hand. She is too proud to let on, but I think she had a *tendre* for him, and she could see well enough it was you he liked. What a tragedy if Penfel has to marry her. She would not be satisfied with Lord John, you must know."

"Don't be foolish, Miss Fenshaw. If you have nothing helpful to say, then be quiet. You are only making things worse by this sort of scandal mongering."

"I don't want her for a sister-in-law!" Kate pouted, and left.

Quilp was commandeered to bear her ladyship company. Penfel and Farber joined Abbie.

"How do you figure he got her away?" she asked. "Does O'Leary have a carriage?"

"He has a gig. It's missing," Farber told her. "I wager he has her hidden in some out-of-the-way spot by now, but someone might have seen them. Before we left the Hall, his lordship sent men out to make queries along the roads in all directions and at the coach stops, though I shouldn't think it likely O'Leary would tackle a public conveyance with a reluctant lady."

"Unless he drugged her or knocked her unconscious, I don't see how he could have accomplished it, even in a private gig," Abbie replied. "I wonder if he used an accomplice. That Sadie, who gave you the ring, Penfel—would she be in on it?"

"I'll see if she is in her tent. If O'Leary went off without her, she might be angry enough to help us."

"I'll poke about and see if any of the other workers are missing," Farber said, and dashed off into the throng.

"What could I be doing to help?" Abbie asked Penfel.

"Come with me. I don't want some hedgebird to carry you off on me. Just go along with whatever I say to Sadie. A little prevarication may be necessary to get her help."

He took her hand and led her to the edge of the fairgrounds, where the performers' tents had been erected. The dancers were in their tent, preparing for their performance. As it was impossible to knock, Penfel just lifted the flap and poked his head inside, causing girlish shrieks and laughter from within and a gasp of disapproval from Abbie.

"Peeping Tom!" the girls screeched. When they recognized who was peeping, the voices settled down to welcome. "Oh, it's you, Penfel!"

"Could I have a word with you, Sadie?"

"Come on in, then. Don't be shy, love."

"This is private," Penfel replied. More giggles and shrieks ensued.

In thirty seconds, a female with brilliant red curls and a face so laden with rouge and powder, it looked like a pretty clown's face emerged from the tent, pulling a green satin dressing gown around her fulsome form. Her smile of welcome dwindled when she saw Penfel was with a lady.

"What is it, then?" she asked in a brassy voice.

133

"I'm looking for O'Leary. Do you know where he is?"

"In his wagon, likely. He ain't here." She sounded genuinely confused. "Is it about the—you know?" Abbie mentally supplied the word "ring."

"Not exactly. One of the girls who is staying at Penfel has disappeared. I think O'Leary has run off with her."

"No! With one of them grand ladies? Not likely. Which one is gone?"

"The brewer's daughter. Very well to grass. Her family has sent her to an expensive ladies' seminary, trying to make a lady of her. O'Leary has been loitering about the Hall, making up to her every chance he gets, and she is not entirely averse. She's a pretty little thing, but of course it is her dowry—twenty-five thousand—that he's after. If he keeps her away for the night, her papa will have little choice but to accept him as a son-in-law."

As he spoke, Sadie's painted face clenched in fury. "So that is what he has been up to, and letting on he was—" She came to a halt, but now that Abbie knew O'Leary's history, she could supply the rest. Let on he was finding out what Penfel Hall had to offer, and how he might best steal it.

"If I don't recover Miss Kirby tonight, then I fear you have seen the last of O'Leary," Penfel continued. "He won't have to run a traveling show once he lands himself an heiress."

Sadie began snorting like a bull. "And him making fun of them fine ladies behind their backs, telling me they was all a parcel of hoity-toity antidotes, and that lady who teaches them the worst of the lot." She cast a darkling glance on Abbie. "No harm meant, I'm sure," she added.

"Do you know where he might have taken her?" Abbie asked.

"His rig is missing," Penfel added.

Sadie stood a moment, undecided. Abbie sensed that Penfel was equally indecisive. After a moment, he made up his mind and spoke.

"Bow Street knows about the rig O'Leary is running," he said. "By morning, O'Leary's cohorts will be locked up."

"He has no cohorts except Larry, the fence who sells the goods in London. He don't come till O'Leary sends for him."

"You all knew he'd changed his name from Brannigan."

"He said he was running away from debts. No harm in that."

Penfel could hardly suppress a grin at this rudimentary notion of ethics. "You were receiving stolen goods."

"Since when is it a crime to accept a little gift from a gent? And that's all I done. He said he'd bought it. The green ring, was it the real thing, then?"

"It was. It's a crime to receive stolen goods. You could serve a long stretch in Bridewell, Sadie. I'll help you get away if you will tell me where O'Leary is."

"It's pretty clear he meant to leave me behind," she said, frowning in concentration as she made her decision. "He did mention once that a duke's girl would have a handsome dot. He never said it was the brewer's chit he had in his eye. That's different. A duke would never marry his chit off to a fellow like O'Leary, but a brewer—O'Leary can act like a gentleman when he wants."

A tense silence grew as Sadie wrung her hands

135

and frowned into the distance, and Abbie and Penfel gazed at each other, silently praying for her help.

"I'll throw in a hundred pounds to see you safely to London," Penfel said, to tip the balance.

"Done!" she said, and stuck out her hand to give Penfel's a shake. She took his elbow and drew him away from the tent, to ensure her betrayal went unheard. "Let us see the color of your gold first." Penfel drew out his purse and counted out a hundred pounds. She stashed it in her bodice, gave it a satisfied pat, and said, "There's an inn just south of Grinstead. The Duck and Dragon, it's called."

Penfel nodded. "I've seen the place. A raffish clientele."

"Highwaymen and smugglers hang about there when the law is after them. They have regular clients as well, but the real money is in hiding coves from the law. I wager that's where he'd take her. He'd not want to go far in an open rig. Mind you, he might be making a dart for Gretna Green. Worse luck to the girl if he is. O'Leary already has a wife in Ireland, or I'd be married to him by now."

"You're well away from him," Abbie said.

"He's not a bad cove, all said," Sadie said, smiling in fond remembrance. "Full of blarney. And generous, like, when he's in his cups." She shook herself to attention. "You don't mind if I take Millie with me, Penfel? You know Millie is like a sister to me."

"Take anyone you like," he said, and gave her a peck on the cheek, while Abbie watched in stern disapproval.

Sadie went back into the tent, and Penfel turned to Abbie.

"I'll take Farber with me. You go back to the Hall

136

with Mama and the others. With luck, I'll be with you in an hour or two."

He took her elbow, and they began working their way toward the group from Penfel Hall.

"Aren't you going to ask me why I substituted Miss Kirby for Susan?" he asked.

"I assume it was to make Sadie jealous. If she had known it was only kidnapping he had in mind, she would not have cooperated."

"Yes, I counted on her jealousy, which is perfectly unfounded, by the way. O'Leary is mad for the wench. No accounting for taste."

"Yet he didn't tell her he planned to kidnap Susan."

"I expect it was a spur-of-the-moment thing. He was angry with me for having duped him. He realized Bow Street was onto his circus lay, so that means of making money was gone. He saw his opportunity to snatch her and demand a handsome reward, and took it. He would have notified Sadie before morning."

"I wonder who O'Leary will demand ransom from, you or the duke."

"I know which of us has more blunt, and it is not me."

"Yes, but on the other hand, it is you he is angry with. He probably knows how much he could get from you. This escapade has already cost you a hundred pounds."

He turned to her and smiled. "A small price to pay for deliverance from a life with Lady Susan, wouldn't you say? That is the alternative, if I don't get her back unharmed, and very soon."

"One could do worse than a dowry of twenty thousand and a handsome, well-born, well-bred wife who possesses common sense."

"You omitted one of the major advantages—lengthy visits at Wycliffe and Elmgrove with 'Papa, the duke.' In fact, interminable visits. The Wycliffes are a close-knit family. No, no, a dowry of twenty million would not be a large enough bribe. Besides, I have other plans in the marriage department. But we shall speak of that later."

Abbie stumbled at that moment, and used it as an excuse for her shortness of breath. Penfel steadied her and gazed down at her, with a small smile twitching the corners of his lips. "Knocked the wind out of you, have I?"

"Certainly not. I stubbed my toe."

"Stub your toe, meet your beau. May I introduce myself, Miss Fairchild?"

"Don't be ridiculous. Your marriage plans are of no interest to me," she said in a breathless voice. "Though I do think you ought to delay any announcement you are planning to make for a month or so, after your recent refusal by Lady Eleanor. Or so the world thinks, at least. The visit was spoken of a good deal."

"You are right, as usual. But I shan't wait that long to make my offer. Be prepared, Miss Fairchild."

"Don't talk like a moonling, milord."

He tilted his head aside and looked down at her. "Do I hear a trace of Lady Susan in that speech? Come, Abbie, show me a smile to cheer me on my way. You know what dark thoughts will be harbored in my poor hollow old head as I fly, *ventre à terre*, to the rescue. A life of odious comparisons with Wycliffe. That's better!" he said, when an uncertain smile peeped out.

"I was just wondering what O'Leary will make of

Lady Susan," she said. "Do you know, I almost pity him."

"Aye, it would serve him right if she accepted him."

"He is already married, according to Sadie."

"He told her so, but I shouldn't be surprised if that is only a ploy to escape parson's mousetrap."

"I thought he was madly in love with Sadie!"

"So he is, this year."

Abbie shook her head. "Men!" she scoffed.

"What would you ladies have to complain about without us?" he asked with a charming smile.

Chapter Fifteen

As soon as Penfel returned Abbie to the group, they all left the meadow. Penfel and Farber hastened on ahead and were just dashing down the road in the curricle when the others reached the Hall. There was no need to ask if Lady Susan had turned up. Sifton's sad face and shaking head told them she had not. As they sat about the saloon, discussing what they had learned from Sadie and worrying, Lord John began to see he was missing out on some fine excitement.

"I ought to have gone with Algie," he said. "He and Farber may need a hand."

Singleton hummed his agreement.

Lady Penfel said, "Dear me, I daresay I ought to go as well. I mean to say, if Susan is in distress, there ought to be a lady there to succor her." She turned an assessing eye on Abbie, who had been searching her mind for some excuse to join Lord John and Singleton.

"I will be happy to go in your place, ma'am," she said at once.

"Thank you, Miss Fairview. At my age, you know, I am not up to such carrying on. So kind."

Lord John objected to this notion. "Algie won't like our drawing Miss Fairchild into it, Mama. You know how he feels about—er, about ladies," he finished lamely.

"I know how it will look to Nettie if her daughter is not shown every consideration!" she retorted. "Wretched girl. How on earth did O'Leary get hold of her?"

Abbie didn't listen to the various suggestions as to how this had been achieved. She was busy deciding what she should take to help Susan in her distress. What if O'Leary had beaten her, even molested her sexually? She would take smelling salts, along with plasters, bandages, and basilicum powder in case of wounds. A blanket or pelisse might come in handy, if her clothing had been ripped.

Lord John sent Sifton off to call the carriage, and Abbie hurried abovestairs to assemble what might be helpful in the rescue. When she returned below, Lord John and Singleton were waiting.

"Going as well," Singleton said, and muttered some incoherent sounds that Lord John translated as meaning Singleton was an excellent man of science, very good with his fists, despite his spectacles.

"I trust you to keep John out of trouble, Miss Fairchild" was Kate's parting shot.

Lady Penfel said more practically, "You have a pistol, Johnnie?"

He brandished a pistol. His joyful "Indeed I have!" said clearly that as far as he was concerned, this night's work was rare sport.

All the ladies went to the door to wave them off. Lord John called, "Spring 'em," to the coach driver, and they were off in a clatter of wheels and a lurch that caused some discomfort to Abbie's neck. The coachman's lively pace jolted them about mercilessly. Through the window, Abbie watched the tall trees sway in the breeze. A fat moon shone benignly, silvering the meadows as the grass shivered.

141

"I say," Lord John exclaimed when they reached the main road, "Does anyone know where we're going?"

"The Duck and Dragon, just south of Grinstead," Abbie replied. "I told the driver."

"The Duck and Dragon!" Lord John's enthusiasm for the project faded. "That's a nasty sort of place, a den of cutthroat thieves, according to rumor."

"What sort of place did you think he would take her?" she asked.

"That sort," Singleton said. Some further mutterings suggested the Duck and Dragon was no place for a lady, meaning Miss Fairchild.

"You wait in the carriage when we get there," Lord John said to Abbie.

After half an hour of jostling that seemed much longer, Lord John pulled the drawstring and the coach drew to a stop.

"The tavern is just around the corner," he said. "It might be wise to leave the carriage here and sneak up on O'Leary on foot."

After a little convincing, Lord John allowed Abbie to accompany them to the inn, with strict instructions that she was not to enter. She carried the blanket over her arm, and in her reticule, the medications. As they turned the corner, the Duck and Dragon came into view. The ancient building listing slightly to the left looked infinitely menacing in the darkness. A business catering to public needs was usually illuminated at night. It was a thatched roof inn of brick and timber, two stories high, with a low doorway and with a railed balcony running around the top story. Perhaps the criminal class had made this haunt their own because it allowed easy escape from a bedroom should the law appear unexpectedly belowstairs. It also had a small forest behind that would hamper capture.

142

As they drew nearer, Penfel appeared from the shadows and accosted them, causing a yelp of fearful surprise.

"Oh, it's only you, Algie!" Lord John said.

"What the devil are you doing here, cawker?" Penfel demanded.

"We came to help you."

"And bringing Miss Fairchild along on such a mission!"

"All Mama's idea."

"In case Lady Susan has been hurt, you know. I have blankets and medications with me," she said, indicating her supplies.

Farber came skulking forward from behind the building, where he had been scouting out the situation.

"He's in there right enough," he said. "His rig's not in the stable—it would be hidden in the spinney behind, but I recognized his nag despite the bootblack he'd used on its forehead to cover the white star. An old trick. I didn't ask any questions. 'Twould only alert the stable hands I'm after him. Considering the importance of the victim, I'm wondering if we oughtn't to call in the local constable and a few recruits to help us."

"The duke would not want any publicity," Penfel said firmly. "We have practically an army here."

"A larger army within," Farber warned. "The tavern is full tonight. If we try to haul O'Leary out, we'll have every man jack of them on our backs."

Singleton lifted his hands, clenched into fists to denote his readiness for battle.

"Is O'Leary actually in the tavern?" Abbie asked. "If he is abovestairs, you might get to his room without alerting the men in the tavern to your presence."

"I tried to look in the window. It has dirty, crinkly glass too thick to make out faces," Farber said. "But I could see the size of the crowd, and it's a full room tonight."

"Does O'Leary know you all by sight?" she asked, "or could one of you go in and see if he's in the tavern?"

"He knows Penfel, of course," Farber said. "I don't know if he's onto me or not."

"I've met him," Lord John said. "He's seen you as well, Singleton."

"Hardly glanced at me. Wouldn't suspect me—only a tutor."

Penfel and Lord John exchanged a questioning look. "He's an excellent man of science," John reminded his brother.

"All right," Penfel said. "Just walk nonchalantly into the tavern and order a small ale, Singleton. See if O'Leary's there. Take a few sips of your ale and get out."

"I will." He squared his shoulders and marched in without a backward glance. Singleton might be afraid to speak, but he obviously had no fear of physical danger.

"A good man, that," Lord John said.

"Does he have a gun?" Penfel asked.

"Er—no. I'm carrying the pistol."

Without further speech, the three men began to move closer to the inn, ready to dash to Singleton's assistance at the first sound of trouble.

Penfel looked over his shoulder and said to Abbie, "Go back to the carriage, Miss Fairchild."

She didn't reply, or move. She just stood waiting, with her heart throbbing in her throat and the blanket over her arm, praying that there would be

144

no shooting. Her only familiarity with the criminal class was a servant who snitched a few pounds from her purse. She had no familiarity at all with the rougher sort who used fists and pistols and clubs.

The men stopped a few yards from the front door, waiting. After a brief interval, Singleton came out, shaking his head to indicate O'Leary was not inside. Thus far, there had been no sign of trouble. It seemed O'Leary had taken Lady Susan to one of the bedchambers, then.

At once a terrible foreboding assailed Abbie. What if O'Leary had molested her? Penfel would have to marry her! Her own reputation would suffer as well. She was in charge of the girls. And with such a scandal hanging over its head, Miss Slatkin's Academy would never be trusted to look after another student.

After a moment's anxiety, Abbie could no longer stand waiting. She crossed the road just as the men separated, going in different directions. Farber remained outside the front door. She ran forward and spoke to him.

"What is happening?"

"O'Leary is not in the tavern. Penfel is clambering up to the balcony to try to get a look in at the bedroom windows. There is no access to the balcony from below. He will have to scamper up one of the posts. The younger lads are waiting behind, one on either side of the inn to catch O'Leary if he makes it down from the balcony. We'll get him this time, ma'am, never you fear."

"But will he already have harmed Lady Susan?"

Farber shook his head sadly. "I fear it is a possibility. O'Leary has a hot eye and a busy hand for the women. Though Lady Susan is not exactly his type."

It seemed a long time they waited, worrying and

watching as Penfel went from window to window, listening and trying to peer through the curtains. When he had made the whole circuit, he clambered down and joined them.

"He may have her in one of those rooms. There is no telling from outside. I'm going in. I'll ask for a room."

Farber looked doubtful. "This is not the sort of establishment that caters to lords."

"I've never been inside. They won't know who I am."

"They'll know you're not their sort!"

Penfel looked offended at this charge of a respectable appearance. "I might pass for a royal scamp, with some little changes to my costume. I've heard our local highwayman, Jack Rasher, dresses like a gentleman. I'll say I've held up a carriage and need a private room for a few days."

"They'll know you're not a local cove."

"True, Jack Rasher doesn't like intruders on his turf. I'll be from another parish. Once I'm inside, I can investigate more thoroughly. Perhaps there are rooms hidden belowstairs or some such thing."

As he spoke, he removed his hat and placed Farber's vastly inferior one on his head. He removed the diamond pin from his cravat, pulled off his cravat, and handed it to Farber. "May I borrow your kerchief?" They exchanged cravat for kerchief. These few modifications altered his appearance slightly, but it was his rakish expression and low accent that perfected the transformation.

" 'Tis hard work being on the scamp lay, never placing your head on the feathers till the sun is out. I wager the coves won't recognize Weston's work," he said, loosening his jacket and squeezing it into wrin-

146

kles to conceal the exquisite cut of London's premier tailor. "I'll need more loot." He pulled his watch from his pocket and detached the chain from his waistcoat. He added watch and chain to his diamond cravat pin, pulled a crested ring from his finger and his purse from his pocket. He looked to Abbie. "Stand and deliver, miss! Your ring and necklace or your life."

She removed the little pearl ring from her finger and the antique necklace with emerald chips from her throat and gave them to him. Now that he was ready to go, she was seized by a terrible fear that she would never see him alive again.

"Would it help if I go with you? I could pretend I'm your—doxy," she said, choking over the low word.

He looked up from his collection of jewelry and grinned. "You wouldn't fool a schoolboy," he said, in his own accents, "but I admire your spirit. Is there any point asking you to return to the carriage?"

"No."

"I'd like to go in with you," Farber said, "but I fear I would give the show away. Those fellows can smell the law a mile away."

"You stay here with Miss Fairchild. If you see O'Leary darting out, grab him."

On this speech, Penfel cocked Farber's hat over his eye, winked at Abbie, and swaggered into the tilting inn to request a very private room for a few days' rustication.

The proprietor, a shifty-eyed man with a vast stomach, was wary. "How did you hear about me?" he asked.

"From a cove in my line of work. I'm not poaching on Jack Rasher's territory, if that's what worries you. I had a spot of trouble just outside Epsom. Fear

147

I may have killed a cove. He didn't want to part with his purse." He patted his pocket that jingled from its contents and smiled.

"I don't need no details. I'm an honest businessman."

"I wouldn't be here if you weren't reliable, now, would I? I'll need a very private room—with a way out, if you know what I mean." As he spoke, he put his hand in his pocket and drew out the jewelry, assessed it as if selecting a piece of the proper value, and returned it to his pocket. "Best pay in cash," he said. "These sparklers are hot." He handed the proprietor a bill of large denomination.

The proprietor examined him a long minute, then nodded and gave him a key. "Back of the storeroom at the end of the corridor, next to the stairs. Behind the stacks of linen, you'll find a door. The room's small—has a bed and washstand. Under the washstand's a trapdoor leading down a flight of stairs to the cellar. The cellar door there only opens from the inside. Safe as churches. There's a bell by the bed. I'll give it a ring if anyone comes asking for you, but there's no need to panic. No one's ever been caught there. You need food, wine?"

"Just a bed," Penfel said, as he didn't want servants going to see he wasn't where he was supposed to be.

He picked up the key, the proprietor directed him down the corridor, and he went toward the linen closet. In the corner, he saw a staircase leading up to the bedchambers. Without even opening the door of the linen closet, he darted up the stairs and began listening at the bedroom doors, opening them if they weren't locked. All the unlocked rooms were empty. The men in the rooms didn't want anyone taking them by surprise. Between listening at keyholes and listening through the walls of the empty rooms, he was soon convinced O'Leary was not in any of the regular bedrooms. The obliging proprietor had arranged some more private accommodation for O'Leary and Lady Susan. If it was as well concealed as his own room, he would have a difficult time finding it.

He was beginning to think Farber must make an official entry. The "honest businessman's" livelihood depended on defending his "guests." He wouldn't hand O'Leary over peacefully. There would be a huge brawl, gunshots, wounds, possibly even a death. The whole affair would be a local scandal by morning, and whispered about in London when the trial began.

And he would have to marry Lady Susan. No, there had to be another way. But as he stood, racking his brains, he couldn't imagine what other way was open to him. And there wasn't a minute to spare. Lady Susan's honor might even now be in terrible jeopardy.

Chapter Sixteen

"I don't believe O'Leary has her abovestairs," Penfel reported to Farber and Abbie when he slipped out the cellar door and met them again outside the Duck and Dragon. "How could he have taken her in if she was protesting? She would have been hollering 'The Duke of Wycliffe' at the top of her lungs. I doubt the proprietor would stand still for that. It's not as if O'Leary is one of his regulars."

"Perhaps she was drugged. He might have let on she was ill," Abbie suggested.

"The inn has some hidden rooms." Penfel described his own hidey-hole to them, which was arranged just as the innkeeper had said.

Farber nodded. "I'd best go in and make it official. We've no time to waste."

Penfel's jaws locked in grim resignation. He could only look his desolation at Abbie, whose eyes mirrored the emotion. She read in his look that his feelings for her were not a passing fancy, not a flirtation, but the beginning at least of true love. Unspoken between them was the knowledge of how this would affect their romance. Abbie hardly knew whether she was more sorry for Penfel, having to spend the rest of his life amid the Wycliffes, or for herself, never seeing him again.

She opened her lips twice, but no words came out. She cleared her throat and said in a strained voice, "O'Leary must be in a room similar to the one you have, Penfel, if only we could find it."

"How do we do that, other than asking the innkeeper where O'Leary is?" Farber asked. "That will make him demmed suspicious."

Penfel's brow furrowed in thought, then he looked up with a beam of hope flashing in his eyes. "Not necessarily. Why could I not claim to be a friend of O'Leary's? Birds of a feather, you know. I'll mention hearing O'Leary's Circus is playing hereabouts, and inquire about my old chum, O'Leary. It can't do any harm to try. I've given the notion I'm fagged and want only my bed, but that is no matter. I'll say I can't sleep."

"Ask for a game of cards!" Abbie exclaimed. "I shouldn't be surprised if they know O'Leary is a Captain Sharp."

"A good idea! I'll go at once. Stand by, Farber, and keep an eye on Johnnie and Singleton to see they don't do something foolish."

Penfel hastened back to the cellar door, which he had propped open to allow himself to reenter his hidey-hole. While Farber and Abbie stood, waiting on nettles, Lord John came creeping silently around the side of the building, wearing a broad grin.

"I believe I've found them!" he whispered.

"Where?" Abbie and Farber demanded in unison.

"There's a wee shack in the woods. I noticed a servant from the inn taking a bottle of wine into the woods, and followed him. He didn't see me. I haven't investigated yet. I thought I'd best tell Penfel. Where is he?"

"He's inside," Farber said. "We'll let him do what

151

he's doing, in case your wee shack is a red herring. Let us go and have a look at it."

Abbie said, "No!" in a firm voice. "We shouldn't all leave. Someone must stay here in case Penfel needs help. You stay, Farber. Lord John and I will investigate and let you know what we learn."

Farber considered her command and said, "Happen you're right. But don't try to apprehend O'Leary. Come back and let me know if he's there."

"Right," Lord John said, and he and Abbie ran off, with Lord John brandishing the pistol.

It was not a look they had so much as a listen. Lord John led the way along a path into the woods, that were black as pitch. The only sounds were the menacing whisper of leaves overhead and the occasional rustle in the grass as a night creature went about its job of seeking food. After a few hundred yards, they came to a small cottage of weathered clapboard. Were it not for a sliver of light around the drawn curtains, it would have been invisible in the darkness of the surrounding forest. Its size suggested it was only one room. They went on tiptoe, making a circuit of the little house, trying for an open curtain to determine who was within.

All the curtains were drawn tightly, but the window at the back was open an inch for ventilation. An echo of voices came from within.

"You will certainly hang if you touch a hair of my head," Lady Susan said, in her usual complacent accents. Abbie was never so glad to hear it in her life. She and John exchanged a triumphant smile, then applied their ears to the raised window to try to gauge the situation within. It did not seem Lady Susan was in any immediate danger.

O'Leary's voice was bored. "I wouldn't touch you

with a pair of tongs, miss. You are about as appealing as a dead spinster."

"That's not what you said yesterday!"

"You ain't the sort that improves on acquaintance."

"The chief magistrate is my uncle. I have two cousins who are Supreme Court judges. Every Runner and constable in the country will be out looking for us. You will hang from the gibbet for this night's work, O'Leary. And incidentally, a duke's daughter is called 'lady,' not 'miss.' "

"Shut up, you shrew."

"Furthermore, my papa is not at Wycliffe or his smaller estate, Elmgrove. He has gone to Dugal Castle, his estate in Scotland, on business. It will be weeks before you could get your ten thousand pounds, even if he ever agreed to give you a penny, which he would not. He is against encouraging crime. If he paid you, not a lady in the land would be safe from such cunning rogues as yourself."

"He ought to pay me for taking you."

"You shan't get a sou. I would like some cocoa, if you please."

"Drink your wine."

"It is horrid, sour stuff. Tastes like vinegar. Papa, the duke, would not allow such an inferior vintage in his cellar. I want cocoa—now."

"Shut up, you demmed clapperjaw."

There was a very brief silence, then Lady Susan spoke again.

"I want something to read. Get me the journal."

Abbie deduced that Lady Susan was not tied up, or she could not drink or manage to read a journal. O'Leary must be holding a gun on her. This could make her rescue even more difficult and dangerous.

In spite of O'Leary's heinous character, Abbie began to feel a smidgen of pity for him.

He apparently handed Susan a journal, for she said in a scoffing tone, "Not that one. It is weeks old."

O'Leary swore off a string of curses. "I'll have to tie you up if I leave."

"If you knew what you were about, you would have brought some laudanum."

"That wasn't necessary, was it, Miss High and Mighty? I don't envy your husband, whoever he turns out to be."

"I don't envy you, when you are caught. Papa—"

Abbie assumed O'Leary had lost patience and gagged her. There was a short silence, then the front door slammed. He must have tied her up as well, or he would not leave her alone.

"He's leaving!" Lord John whispered.

They darted around to the front of the little building just as O'Leary headed down the path, muttering to himself.

"He's going to the inn!" Abbie whispered. "He'll see Penfel! And he has a gun! Go and warn Farber, John."

"You'll rescue Susan?"

"Yes, of course. Hurry!"

Lord John scampered off after O'Leary, and Abbie tried the front door. It was not locked. She peered in to make sure O'Leary didn't have an accomplice before entering. When she saw the situation was safe, she walked into a little cottage that lacked only a fire in the hearth to make it cozy. It had a stove, a cupboard, a table holding a bottle of wine and two glasses, with chairs and a horsehair sofa in the corner. Lady Susan was tied to a straight-backed

154

wooden chair at the table. She had been gagged with O'Leary's cravat. Her eyes were not rolling in distress, nor was there a sign of a tear. Abbie rushed forward and untied her, then Lady Susan ungagged herself.

"It took you long enough!" was her first speech.

Abbie grabbed her hand and hurried her from the cottage.

"There is no rush now," Lady Susan said. "I expect the law is waiting to take O'Leary into custody."

"Yes. Susan, are you all right? He didn't—"

She stopped and regarded Abbie with a curious frown. "No, he didn't touch me—in that way, I mean. He didn't try to kiss me, or maul me, though he had me alone, at his mercy. Why do you think that is, Miss Fairchild?" She sounded almost offended. "I sensed he is a passionate man."

"Oh, his mind was only on business."

"Yes, of course that's it," she said, but she still wore her frown.

Abbie threw a blanket over her shoulders, more to be rid of it than anything else, for Susan's clothing was not much disheveled, and they continued on their way. Lady Susan displayed neither gratitude nor curiosity as to how she had been found and rescued. When they reached the back of the inn, they saw Singleton standing over an inert body on the ground. He removed his spectacles from his pocket and placed them on his nose.

"Recognized him," he said, tossing his head at O'Leary. "Milled him down."

Lady Susan just looked at O'Leary, sniffed, lifted her nose in the air, and walked away. She didn't thank Singleton, or even look at him.

"Well done, Singleton! I'll get Farber," Abbie said,

and hastened to the front of the inn, where Farber was pacing and staring at the tavern window. She gasped out the story of Susan's rescue. "Penfel hasn't come out?" she asked.

"Nay, do you think we ought to fetch him?"

"Singleton will do it," she said, as he was obviously a stranger to fear.

They went around to the back of the inn. O'Leary was put into manacles and stood silent, with a sneering smile on his face, but a desperate gleam in his eyes. He looked at Lady Susan, then turned to Abbie and smiled.

"I think I chose the wrong lady," he said.

"Miss Fairchild has no money!" Susan said. That curious frown was back on her haughty face.

"There's more to life than money and titles, milady."

"Idiot!" she scoffed, then she turned to study Miss Fairchild, wondering what O'Leary meant.

Abbie outlined what Penfel was doing inside the inn.

Without being asked, Singleton said, "I'll fetch him." He walked off and returned a moment later with Lord Penfel, both of them unharmed.

Apparently, Singleton had not found words to make the situation clear. "You mean it's all over?" Penfel asked, staring from Lady Susan to O'Leary to Abbie.

"It is, and not a shot fired," Farber said with satisfaction.

Penfel took an involuntary step toward Abbie, then recalled his duty and made the necessary inquiries for Susan's well-being first. She was not the sort to minimize her suffering. O'Leary listened, shaking his head in disbelief, while she outlined the trials of her capture and incarceration.

156

"I should have brought a muzzle" was his only comment.

"Most unfortunate," Penfel said to Lady Susan, placing a protective arm around her unyielding shoulder. "I'm extremely sorry this happened while you were under my protection. I shall endeavor to make it up to you, Susan."

Lady Susan nodded her forgiveness.

This done, Penfel joined Abbie. "It seems Singleton is the hero of the piece. I had hoped I might play the role, to impress you." His hands clasped hers in a strong, warm grip. He was encouraged by the directness of her gaze back at him. All her uncertainty had evaporated. She smiled with the full warmth and love she felt for him.

"Heroes are only for a day," she said, thinking of her uncle, whose one heroic effort grew so dull when it had to last him a lifetime.

"How did you get so wise?"

"From living with a hero," she said.

"A mischievous statement!" he exclaimed, but his expression held more pleasure than jealousy. "I trust this is the colonel you are referring to. You must tell me all about him. It occurs to me we don't know much about each other."

They became aware that Farber was jiggling from foot to foot in impatience. He called, "Let us get off from this place before the lads inside realize what has happened and come after us."

It was decided that Penfel and Farber would deliver O'Leary to the roundhouse in the curricle, to await his hearing in the morning. Lord John and Singleton would take the ladies back to Penfel Hall.

Lady Susan had a great deal to say about how abominably O'Leary had treated her—lying to her, rough handling, jiggly ride in a gig, smelly old blanket, bad wine, being tied, gagged, and held at gunpoint—but not a word about how she had fallen into his hands.

"How did he get hold of you?" Lord John asked, when she stopped to draw a breath.

After a little hesitation, she began uncertainly. "It was at—at the refreshment booth," she said. "I mentioned how sour the lemonade was. O'Leary overheard me and said he had some better refreshment in his wagon. Champagne, actually." Her nervousness lessened as she continued her tale. "Naturally, I refused to enter his wagon, but I agreed to accept a glass if he brought it out to me. He hadn't the wits to put some laudanum in it—imagine! However, while I was drinking it, he pulled my arms behind my back and dragged me inside. He tied me up and left me there while he went to bring his gig to the back door. He dumped me in the bottom of it with a dirty old blanket over my head, and drove off."

"Did no one see you?" Abbie asked. "O'Leary's wagon is in plain view of the circus."

"He chose a moment when no one was looking."

"Could you not have called for help? Someone would have heard you and gone to your rescue."

"It—it was all done very quickly. Papa will be furious when he hears."

The story had to be told again in full, several times, when they reached Penfel Hall. Kate and Annabelle hung on her every word, oohing and ahing as she described being dumped in the wagon with a filthy blanket over her. "And a gag in my mouth," she added, looking around nervously. No one questioned her tale, however.

"How horrid!" Annabelle exclaimed.

158

"I wish it had been me," Kate said. "It sounds wonderfully exciting, just like a novel."

"At least there is one good thing," Lady Susan said. "I shan't have to return to Miss Slatkin's boring old school now that I am engaged. I shall just stay here until Penfel and I get married. I daresay Papa will have to sanction the match. He won't like that Lady Eleanor business."

Everyone stared at her. It was Lady Penfel who said what they were all thinking. "Has Algie proposed?"

"Of course. And, in any case, it is taken for granted when a lady has been so dreadfully abused at the hands of her protector, he must marry her. I trust Penfel will do his duty. Indeed, he has already said he will make it up to me."

Kate looked a question at Abbie, who sat, stunned. She knew Penfel had exerted every effort to avoid having to offer for her, but if Lady Susan insisted, it would be difficult to get out of the match.

"How nice," Lady Penfel said in a weak voice, but her fallen face said "Catastrophe!" as clearly as if she had shouted the word.

Singleton muttered something that sounded like "Rubbish" into his collar.

Abbie became aware that all eyes were on her. How did they know she and Penfel cared for each other? She cleared her throat and said, "We have not wished you well on your engagement, Lady Susan. I hope you will be very happy."

"Penfel must write to Papa tomorrow and ask his permission. Under the circumstances, there can be no question of his refusing. The dancing party Penfel plans can be our engagement party."

Having decided these details unilaterally, she said, "We shall be leaving for Wycliffe as soon as Papa

159

returns, Lady Penfel. You are perfectly welcome to come with us, if you are free."

"Very kind of you." Lady Penfel stared hard at Abbie and said, "We shall see, Susan. We shall see."

Chapter Seventeen

Lady Susan soon retired to her chamber with a paregoric draft to recover from her ordeal. Kate and Annabelle, hoping to hear more details of her kidnapping (and more importantly, her approaching marriage) before the draft took effect, accompanied her abovestairs. During the intervening hour until Penfel returned, those remaining in the saloon had plenty to keep the conversation lively, yet the hour seemed very long.

"Go to Wycliffe, indeed!" Lady Penfel snorted. "I would as lief go to court and watch old Queen Charlotte stuff snuff up her nose. Both places are mausoleums."

"I still don't see how O'Leary got at Susan," John said.

"It would take more than ten thousand pounds to convince me to entertain her again!" his mama said.

When at last Penfel returned, he was alone. Farber had remained behind in town to deal with O'Leary's incarceration.

"Congratulations!" Lady Penfel cried, when her son entered, smiling.

"You mistake the matter, Mama. I am not the hero of the evening. It is Singleton who merits the title," he replied, bowing in Singleton's direction. Singleton, hiding behind his spectacles, blushed and made strange gurgling sounds in his throat.

Penfel's eyes turned to Abbie. There, where he expected a warm welcome, he saw only a travesty of a smile.

"No one said anything about hero, gudgeon," his mama said. "I am speaking of your betrothal to Susan."

"Betrothal!"

"Aye. Whatever you said to the chit, she has taken the notion you want to marry her—or have to. I daresay it is all one and the same to her. You are to write to Dugal Castle tomorrow for Wycliffe's blessing. We were given to understand that under the circumstances, His Grace will agree, even if you are only a lowly earl."

"But—" He turned in confusion from his mama to Abbie, who just looked her compassion. "But that's impossible! Damme, the reason I was so eager to find her is so I wouldn't have to marry her. One of the reasons," he added, when he realized what had slipped out. He sunk into a chair and drew his hand over his eyes to think.

"What we require is a plan to give her a disgust of you," Lady Penfel said. "That should not prove too difficult. A worthier suitor would turn the trick. A duke—even a marquess would do."

"Who would have her?" Lord John asked, in a rhetorical spirit.

"There is that," his mama agreed, nodding.

Penfel removed his fingers from his eyes and said, "I don't see why I must marry her. No one knows of the kidnapping, save the few of us here and Farber. He'll not tell anyone."

Lady Penfel shook her bronze curls. "Oh, for the

optimism of youth! The whole world will know it when O'Leary's case comes to court. And even if we could keep it under cover, she *was* ill treated while under your roof, Algie. She knows it, and the duke will soon hear of it. One hopes to see her children avoid the mistakes that made her own life so miserable, but there is no getting away from it. You will have a perfectly wretched marriage, as I had."

Lord John, who had been massaging his chin, suddenly spoke up. "What if Algie were already engaged?"

"Lady Eleanor has already turned him down," his mama reminded him.

"I was not thinking of Lady Eleanor. What of Miss Fairchild?"

Lady Penfel could never recall Abbie's name correctly, but she recognized it when she heard it. Like the others, she turned and examined Abbie with interest.

"An excellent notion, but alas, it would not fadge. You must know a duke's daughter takes precedence over a schoolmistress. Susan—and the duke—would insist Algie jilt Miss Fairview and marry Susan instead. The only way your stunt would work is if he were already married to Miss Fairview, and he ain't. Are you, Algie?" she asked hopefully.

"Of course not!" he replied, and looked an apology at Abbie. "Miss Fairchild would have something to say about that means of rescuing me in any case."

Abbie found herself doing an imitation of Singleton. An inchoate, demurring sound issued from her throat.

"I don't suppose we could bribe O'Leary to say he had his way with her and make him marry her?" was

163

Lady Penfel's next suggestion. "We would have to let on he is some sort of Irish gentleman, if that is not a contradiction in terms. But that would be a cruel stunt to play on an innocent thief."

Tea was served. After discussing the matter for some time without finding a solution, Lady Penfel rose and said, "Well, it is a knotty problem to be sure. Perhaps if we all sleep on it, someone will come up with an answer. I am for the feather tick. We'll discuss it again tomorrow before you write to Wycliffe, Algie."

Lord John, who was attuned to romance, sensed that Algie wished to be alone with Miss Fairchild, and left, taking Singleton with him.

When Abbie and Penfel were alone, he rose and sat beside her on the sofa. They exchanged a long, deep gaze, then without speaking, he took her hand, lifted it to his lips, and held it there a long moment. In the silent room, Abbie listened to the longcase clock tick away the seconds and thought, I shall treasure this moment forever. It is the closest I shall ever be to Algie.

"I'm sorry, love," he said in a soft, wistful tone.

"It's not your fault," she replied, fighting back the gathering tears.

He batted away her objection. "I am sorry for all the things I didn't say to you when I had the chance; things I have wanted to say since the first moment I saw you, glaring at me at the circus, but it seemed too soon then. And now it is too late."

"I'm happy to know you wanted to say them at least."

"Would you have accepted an offer?"

"You know I would, after a proper amount of vacillating."

"I am happy to know that, too." He frowned at their intertwined fingers as they sat together, each thinking sad thoughts. Then he suddenly looked up. "Do you know, we never did learn how O'Leary got hold of Susan."

"She was at the refreshment stall, complaining of the lemonade. He offered her champagne. She went to his wagon—not into it, but to the door. He hustled her inside when no one was looking, trussed her up, and put her in his gig."

"How does it come no one saw him snatch her? His wagon is right in the open."

"She says he did it when no one was looking."

"I wonder . . ."

"What?"

"If that is how it happened. It was a terrible chance for O'Leary to take, snatching her so publicly. He is usually a deal more circumspect in his criminal doings. Did she ever say anything about him?"

"She did mention a few times that he was handsome. 'One of those irresistible rogues,' she called him. Kate says they were talking together a moment this afternoon. In fact, she had what Spadger calls a *billet doux*, though it may have been a letter from her mama. When we were listening outside the cottage window, I thought she sounded a little put out that he had not molested her. In fact, she chided him that he should have used laudanum, and he said something about its not being necessary. That sounds as though she had gone willingly. You don't think—No, she would never have agreed to accompany him to a low inn."

"No, she'd never do that. This is Susan we're talking about after all."

"She holds herself pretty high, but—do you remember when your mama was saying every lady ought to have a flirtation before she marries? No, you were not there at the time, but somehow O'Leary's name came up, and your mama and Susan agreed that O'Leary would make a charming flirt. I believe Susan had been flirting with him. In her innocence, she would have no idea how dangerous a rogue like O'Leary could be."

"Do you think she might have set up a rendezvous and gone into his wagon willingly?"

Abbie considered it a moment. "She might have, not realizing the danger. She thinks she is above the world because of her papa."

"That would explain the mystery of how he abducted her in front of a few hundred people. She went to meet him willingly, and once he had driven her to some lonely spot, he tied her up and took her to the Duck and Dragon."

"Even if that is true, it would not exonerate you from responsibility for her welfare while she was living under your roof."

Penfel gave a quizzing grin. "Not entirely, but the duke demands perfection from his litter. It would make a very large club to hold over her head, would it not?"

"Oh, my! If 'Papa, the duke' heard she had so far betrayed her family—and with a mere commoner— he would likely put her into a convent." She stopped and frowned. "That is why she has decided to badger you into having her, Penfel! She is afraid the truth will come out, and she will be disgraced."

"I am happy to know she prefers me to disgrace and a life in a nunnery!" he said, offended.

Abbie gave him an indulgent smile. "Do you know, I am coming to like her a little, now that she has revealed some human weakness."

"I will like her a deal more when I am out from under the threat of having to marry her."

The longcase clock in the corner emitted two tinny chimes. They both looked at it, then at each other, remembering their former conversation. Penfel seized her fingers and squeezed them. "Two o'clock, our witching hour." As he spoke, his arms went around her, pulling her against him. When he spoke again, his voice was burred with love. "We are now old friends, Abbie. And as you have already admitted, you would marry me if I were free . . ."

His head came down. Abbie didn't lift hers, but she didn't draw back, either. She gazed into the glittering darkness of his eyes a moment, as if mesmerized, and waited for the touch of his lips. At the first gentle brush, her heart leapt and began palpitating strangely. She felt her lips quiver in nervousness against his. When she shyly looped her arms around his neck, her fingers trembled.

Then he firmed her lips with his, and the kiss deepened inexorably, inevitably, as if her whole life she had been waiting for this moment. Warm fingers moved over the vulnerable nape of her neck, then slid down to feel the pulse throb in her throat, while his other hand pressed her ever more tightly against him, molding her feminine softness against him. A golden glow suffused her, spreading from her chest to her head, to make her giddy with new sensations.

She lowered her arms to his waist to hold him

more tightly, savoring the hard masculine strength of his body. So this was love, this hungry, infinite yearning for another, that seemed almost a part of oneself. All that rubbish she had heard disseminated by her own teachers and had passed on to her girls in turn was nonsense. Love had nothing to do with respect or esteem. It was a visceral imperative that she could no more deny than she could deny breathing. And it was lovely.

After a long embrace, Penfel raised his head and just gazed at her, with his two hands palming her cheeks, while one of his slow, lazy smiles worked its way down from his eyes to move his lips.

She waited to hear what he would say at this crucial moment. The words "I love you" seemed appropriate, but she would let him speak first.

"Pity she took that sleeping draft," he said.

Abbie gave him a dewy-eyed blink. "Sleeping draft?" she asked in confusion.

"Susan. I am eager to make myself entirely eligible. A quasi-betrothal is like my quasi-viscountcy. Something may come along to put an end to it. The only end I want to our betrothal is a marriage."

"How can we be engaged? It would be quasi-bigamy!" She gave him a chiding look. "And besides, you haven't asked me. Not properly."

"Miss Fairchild! I trust you are not the sort of lady who leads a fellow on and jilts him!" She pouted. "Oh, very well. Miss Fairchild, I love you madly. No, I can do better than that. I love you to the edge— nay, the deepest depths of delirium. Will you do the honor to be my wife, providing I can divest myself of my other fiancée?"

"That's better. I am happy to see romance is not dead. Yes, milord, I shall marry you, providing you can be rid of Lady Susan, and providing my uncle agrees to let me marry a man who is not an officer, and has never been to India."

Wrapped up in each other, they did not hear the sounds in the hallway. Although it was very late, Sifton had not retired. He came to the doorway, smiled his approval at what he saw, then uttered a discreet cough.

"Mr. Farber is here, your lordship. He saw the lights in the saloon and came tapping to see if you were up and about. Shall I ask him to return tomorrow?" he asked, with a roguish twinkle in his eye.

"No, show him in."

Farber entered apologetically. "Well, he is booked and locked up right and tight. I have had his wagon searched. He has still half a dozen purloined items in his strongbox, and the address of a certain Larry Wideman who acts as his fence. We can get him on the robberies right enough, but I am a little concerned about the kidnapping. He swears on the Bible, Lady Susan went to his wagon on her own accord. In fact, she agreed to go for a ride in his gig. Of course he kidnapped her, but she made the first overture. If he says that at the Old Bailey, the lady's reputation will be ruined."

This startling news was met with a wide grin.

"Excellent, Farber! Then, we shall forget any charge of kidnapping."

"We may, but O'Leary swears he'll tell his story to the journals. Of course she'll deny it, though it is hard to see how he got her whisked off without anyone seeing him. He has a *billet doux* he says was written by her, agreeing to meet him at his wagon. It is written on her crested stationery. Any chance he might have pinched the paper?"

"Not a chance. She keeps it in her bedchamber," Abbie said.

Farber nodded. "It sounded like a schoolgirl's ranting. She admitted her heart was engaged, but that she could never be his because of her family, and they must be brave. She suggests that she might meet him to discuss it. I daresay that is what he was after, to make the kidnapping easier. If the note is not a forgery, it will blacken the lady's reputation. That *billet doux* is his trump card, and he is playing it for all it is worth."

"What is he after?" Penfel inquired. "He can hardly expect to go scot-free."

"He's trying to save his neck. Even without a charge of kidnapping a duke's daughter, the string of robberies is enough to see him hung."

"I'll see what I can do. Drop a note to the attorney general, or as a last resort to Lord Eldon, the Chancellor of the Exchequer, hinting that a duke's daughter is involved, and any easing of the sentence would be appreciated. No need to name names. They will know what duke's daughter is visiting Penfel. My sisters will see to that. Those London worthies won't want to offend Wycliffe, whatever about me. Something can be arranged, some decrease in O'Leary's sentence."

"I'll hie me back to town and tell him, then, for he was threatening to send for a London journalist and give them his story."

"I'll start the machinery in motion right away, and have an arrangement by tomorrow. But if he breathes a word of all this to anyone, the deal is off."

"He realizes it. O'Leary is up to every rig in town. Well, I'm off, then."

"I shall see you and O'Leary tomorrow."

Farber left, well pleased with the arrangement. Either way, his pockets would be jingling, and he wasn't eager to see O'Leary hang for helping himself to a few baubles from those who could well afford to lose them.

"I should let you get a few hours' sleep," Penfel said to Abbie, when they were alone once more.

Hand in hand, they walked to the bottom of the staircase. Sifton, who was locking the front door and beginning to blow out the lights, disappeared discreetly into the butler's room. In the throes of their love, they didn't want to part.

"I still haven't showed you the da Vinci cartoons," Penfel said.

"And I have not arranged when I am to paint your mama."

"And your fiancé. There will be plenty of time for both after we're married."

She looked at him trustingly. "We will be married, won't we, Algie?"

"That is the first time you have called me Algie. Yes, we will be married, my darling. By hook or by crook. I don't mean to lose you. It would be too bad if I, who have always championed true love, should fall victim to a loveless match. I have always gone scrambling for cover at the first indication of being snared. If some call me a lecher or a flirt, that is the cause. How can you know whether you care for a lady until you know her? How can you get to know her without some advance in friendship? Alas, those initial steps can be taken for a commitment, so one has to dilute the message by pursuing two or three friendships in tandem. And suddenly a gentleman finds himself labeled a gazetted flirt. All I ever wanted was—you."

171

Then he kissed her again, reluctantly letting her go. She continued abovestairs with stars in her eyes, to be brought down to earth by Spadger, who was lurking in the doorway for "a word in private" with Miss Fairchild.

Chapter Eighteen

"What is it, Spadger?" Abbie asked, trying to conceal her impatience. She just wanted to go to bed and think about her newly found love.

"It is Lady Susan, miss."

Abbie's impatience rose to fear. "What's happened to her?"

"She's sleeping like a babe *now*," Spadger said, imbuing the "now" with awful overtones. "She was drowsy-like after taking that sleeping draft. The girls were quizzing her about O'Leary and Penfel, as girls will do, you know." She paused for dramatic effect before making her announcement. "The truth of the matter is, she let out that she went calling on O'Leary, if you please! And went willingly for a spin in his gig, too, with no duress at all."

"She actually made the first move?"

"Can you credit the brass of her? Lady Susan, of all people. Her nice as a nun's hen, or so she would have us believe. And blaming it all on her ladyship. Lady Penfel, I mean. She said her ladyship told her that young ladies should have a flirtation with some devil's kin like O'Leary before they got married, so she took her chance while she was here—she knew well enough her own papa would never allow it—and that is how she came to get herself kidnapped. 'Twas all arranged by *billet doux*. I knew by her sly smile when I saw her conning that little letter this afternoon that it had to do with a man.

"It seems he has been making love to her on the sly. She admits sending him off a note, and he sent her one back, wrapped around a stone, through her window. He wrote that he would be waiting for her at his wagon this evening. Mind you, she only agreed to a little spin in his rig. Much as she knows, she don't know a thing about men, now, does she?

"And now his lordship having to marry her, when it is plain as a pikestaff it is yourself he has feelings for. Or so Miss Fenshaw says. It's a shame and a caution." She directed a sly, quizzing look at Miss Fairchild, her beady eyes asking if this could possibly be true. Abbie's blush was all the confirmation she needed.

"Well, that is a very shocking story," Abbie said. "I only hope she remembers it in the morning."

"The girls won't let her forget it, never you fear. They were gossiping about it for an hour in Miss Fenshaw's room before they went to sleep. I cannot help feeling something ought to be done about it. The mischief in it is that it was her ladyship's bad advice that set Lady Susan off, so in a manner of speaking the Penfels are to blame."

"I shall discuss it with Lord Penfel in the morning. Thank you for telling me, Spadger." To Miss Spadger's amazement, Abbie reached down and kissed her cheek.

Spadger's story gave Abbie hope through a long night, most of which she spent wide awake, thinking.

Lady Susan was up bright and early in the morning, but no earlier than Abbie and the other girls. Abbie went into her room while Spadger was brushing Susan's hair.

"Do you have something you would like to tell me, Lady Susan?" she asked.

"No plans for my wedding can be made until I have heard from Papa," she replied. She did not look up at Abbie, but fiddled with the ribbons on her dress.

Spadger gave a snort and a hard tug on the brush. Susan looked up then, but the harsh words on her lips died aborning. She looked at the two stern-faced ladies staring at her, and blushed.

After a moment's silence, she looked up at Abbie's reflection in the mirror. "Kate told you," she said. "Well, it is true. I did exchange notes with O'Leary. I called on him and went for a drive with him, but it is Lady Penfel's fault. She said I should have a little flirtation with him. How was I to know he would kidnap me?"

"I have heard you instruct the other girls on more than one occasion that a lady takes the blame for her own errors," Abbie said with a chiding look. "Lady Penfel's advice was foolish," she allowed, "but that is not to say Lord Penfel should pay the price for it. You know he doesn't love you, Lady Susan, nor do you love him."

"People like us don't marry for love, Miss Fairchild," she said proudly. "He is eligible, and I am a good match." Then, as they watched, Susan's stiff face crumpled like a starched collar caught in the rain. She buried her face in her hands and began to bawl.

Abbie went to her and patted her heaving shoulders, trying to comfort her.

After a moment, Susan looked up with tears running down her cheeks. "Oh, I don't want to marry him, Miss Fairchild! He is not at all the sort of gentleman I care for. He would not fit in at Wycliffe. He is too—trivial. You know what I mean, always joking and laughing when he should be serious. And his mama! She was a friend of Mama years ago, I know, but she must have changed greatly. What would Papa, the duke, make of her? But what will Papa say if I refuse? I'm ruined! Ruined! Oh, I wish I were dead."

"Rubbish," Abbie said. She felt as if a weight had fallen from her heart, allowing it to soar. Susan didn't want to marry Penfel. That was all she needed to know. "Everyone makes mistakes. No one knows what happened but we few here at the Hall, and we won't tell."

"Not a word will pass these lips, milady!" Spadger promised, and clamped her lips together to make clear her good intentions.

"Papa will know when the case goes to court."

"That aspect of the case need not go to court. If you are willing to overlook it, you may be sure O'Leary will not have his lawyer mention it."

"But Farber knows."

"Penfel will handle Farber."

Susan turned around in her chair and looked up at Abbie, with hope shining in her pale eyes. "No one at the inn saw me. He took me straight to the cabin. Do you think—"

"I believe Penfel can arrange something."

"There is one other thing," Susan said. "I wrote O'Leary a note—If there is some way I could recover it, I would be very grateful."

"I'll speak to Al—er, Lord Penfel this minute," Abbie said, and dashed downstairs.

Penfel was at the table, alone. She ran up to him,

put both arms around his neck, and placed a loud kiss on his cheek. He tried to pull her onto his lap, but she pulled back, laughing.

"And good morning to you, too, Miss Fairchild," he said, rising. She lightly pushed him back into his chair and sat beside him.

"It is done!" she cried. "Lady Susan has admitted everything. Did you write to those important gentlemen in London?"

"I sent a footman off with the letters last night. Well, early this morning. I requested immediate action. We should hear today."

"Susan admitted the whole to Kate and Annabelle last night. She did write to O'Leary and called on him, the minx. And she doesn't want to marry you at all. That is the best part of it. She thinks you are trivial."

He first looked offended. "The Earl of Penfel, Baron Rutcliffe and quasi-Viscount Chance trivial?" Then he shrugged. "Perhaps she is right. I never cared much for the baron myself, but as to Lord Penfel, he is unexceptionable. I do not consider triviality my best feature! A minor virtue at best."

"Idiot!" Abbie said, and went to the sideboard to fill her plate. "Oh, and if you could recover Lady Susan's *billet doux*, she would be extremely relieved."

"I intended to include its return in the bargain. It would be bound to resurface when the duke picks Susan's husband. I shall sell it to the gentleman for a couple of hundred thousand pounds. It will be an easy out for him."

His grin told her he was joking. As other members of the party straggled in, they were brought up-to-date on how matters were progressing. Kate and

177

Annabelle had spoken with Lady Susan before coming down.

"We told her it wasn't right to make Lord Penfel marry her," Kate said.

"Yes indeed. Only see how horrid Lady Penfel turned out," Annabelle added. Singleton made a warning choke in his throat. She looked at him and said, "I don't mean her funny hair and gowns. I am talking about how unhappy she has been all these years. She said so herself, so what is the harm in repeating it?"

"What harm indeed?" John asked. "I like a lady who calls a spade a spade, and a loony a loony."

"Well, I don't think Lady Penfel is loony for wanting to be happy," Kate said. "And you should not speak so disrespectfully of your mama, John."

A much chastened Lady Susan was the last to come to the table. Her chin, usually held high, rested on her collarbone. She was accompanied by Lady Penfel, who was smiling at the girl for the first time since her arrival.

"Lady Susan has something she would like to say to you, Algie," she said, nudging Susan forward.

Lady Susan wore her dutiful face. "I am sorry, Penfel, but I fear I cannot marry you after all. I hope you will not be too disappointed. You haven't written to Papa yet, have you?"

"No, not yet," he replied, trying to conceal his glee beneath a grave countenance.

"Good. And you mustn't breathe a word to Slats!" she added to Kate and Annabelle. "Promise!"

"Not a word," they agreed.

Lady Susan was flattered to death to find herself the center of Kate's and Annabelle's friendly attention. They had always respected her elevated social

178

position, but now she felt they actually liked her. They were treating her as one of themselves, as a friend, and after she had made a fool of herself. How kind they were! The unusual acceptance made her cheeks pink with pleasure. She actually laughed, and didn't deliver a single lecture during the whole breakfast.

After they had eaten, the girls went gossiping off together, merry as grigs.

Lady Penfel looked around the table and smiled. "Well, it did her a world of good to heed my advice. All she needed was a little wickedness in her life, poor girl. She looks better already, with a smile instead of that wretched Wycliffe poker face. Would it not be odd if you fell in love with her after all, Algie, and we all going to such pains to free you from her?"

"Very odd, indeed, Mama," he agreed, with a laughing eye at Abbie.

"Mind you before you go cropping out into a proposal, don't forget there is still Wycliffe and all those boring relatives to be considered."

"To say nothing of Miss Fairchild," Penfel added.

"But she would not be accompanying Susan after the gel leaves school." She regarded Abbie critically. "And really Miss Fairychild is not so bad, once one gets used to her."

"Would it not be odd if Algie fell in love with Miss Fairchild?" Lord John suggested, with a mischievous twinkle in his eyes.

"At least we need not worry about that! I trust he has learned his lesson," her ladyship said, and began to eat her gammon and eggs.

She realized, after a little pause, that her sons were laughing at her. "What are you two whelps snickering about? Very unattractive to see grown men giggling like schoolgirls. What is so humorous, pray?"

Strangely, it was Mr. Singleton who undertook to explain the matter, in his own abbreviated fashion. "Penfel—Miss Fairchild—April and May."

Her ladyship squinted up at Abbie's blushing face and nodded. "She'll do. You parcel of whelps will need a stern lady to keep you in line. I have done the best I can with them, Miss Fairly. Age wants ease. Now it is up to you."

Penfel was busy the next day wrapping up the details of the O'Leary business. Lady Susan's letter was returned to her and burned with great ceremony in her grate, with Kate and Annabelle looking on. Lord Eldon proved amenable in the matter of moderating O'Leary's sentence for robbery. As well, there was the circus to be got rid of. With the manager in jail, it promised to be a daunting task.

Sadie Hutchins heard the story of O'Leary's arrest before she had got beyond the village. She immediately returned and dashed off a note to Lord Penfel requesting him to call on her at the tent, where she suggested a means of disposing of the circus to their mutual advantage.

"Seems a shame to bust up the show. You wouldn't believe what a lot of work it is getting a thing like this together. Elephants and bears don't grow on trees. And there is a decent living in it, even without the ken smashing. So here is what I suggest. I run the show until O'Leary gets out of Newgate. I can talk him into agreeing. That way, we can all keep our jobs, and you don't have elephants and tigers running about your estate, scaring the servants and horses to death."

"I approve, but I really have nothing to say about

180

it, Sadie. You'll have to discuss it with O'Leary. Take a lawyer along to see it is done legally. That is my advice."

"I will, then. We'll be out of here by the weekend, if you can put up with us that long."

"It has been my pleasure, Sadie."

He hastened back to the Hall to see how preparations for the girls' dancing party were progressing. His mama and Abbie were in the ballroom, overseeing the placement of large baskets of flowers and two dozen bentwood chairs around the walls for the older guests.

"We have chosen well, Algie," Lady Penfel said to her son. "Addie will make us a dandy mistress." Penfel cast a wan, apologetic smile on his beloved. It seemed hard that, having reached a first-name basis with Abbie, his mama was now butchering it, as well as her last name.

His mama continued, "I have been telling her how we like things done at our little parties, and she has agreed to stay and do the work while I take a nip down to the circus. I am wondering if I could not borrow the tiger to sit at my feet for my portrait."

"Fine, Mama. Where is Susan?" he asked.

"The youngsters are in the attic, rigging themselves out as pirates and queens and soldiers. We have decided to have a second party before they leave and make it a masquerade do. I want to wear my 'Cleopatra after Actium' outfit. I don't want you or Johnnie wearing that set of scarlet regimentals in the attic, or Susan will go tumbling into love with you. I feel it was O'Leary's Circus uniform that got to her. A man in uniform always works his way with the ladies. Well, if you don't need me here, Annie, I

181

shall run along." She pulled a rose from a bouquet to stick in her curls and left, humming.

"The difficulty of remembering your name will be over once you are Lady Penfel," Algie said, by way of apology.

"Stoopid! How can she call me Lady Penfel when she is called that? I don't really care what she calls me, Algie, as long as she likes me."

"How could she not?" he asked, gazing into her eyes. A smile moved the corners of his lips. "You are relieving her of the onerous duty of watching the servants work, thus freeing her to run down to the circus and buy the tiger. Of course she loves you."

Chapter Nineteen

Penfel and Abbie were not so gauche as to announce their engagement hard on the heels of Susan's difficulties, but there was a whiff of it in the air. On the evening of the dancing party, Lady Susan instructed Spadger to attend to Miss Fairchild's toilette first. Miss Fenshaw had offered to do Susan's hair.

"That was thoughtful of Susan. A real lady, give her that," Spadger said, as she arranged Abbie's chestnut curls in an attractive bundle on top of her head. "When will you be leaving Miss Slatkin, Miss Fairchild, if you don't mind my asking?"

"I shall notify her immediately upon my return, and give her time to find someone to replace me."

"She'll never believe it. Won't the other schoolmistresses stand up and cheer to hear such a one as themselves can nab a lord? Just like a penny novel, innit? Not to say you were ever really like the rest of them. A very superior lady. Miss Slatkin herself always said so, and I'm sure I agreed. Here, let me fasten up your gown, miss. I fancy you'll be wanting a dresser when you are a grand lady?"

"I suppose I will. I never thought of it."

" 'Twould be nice to have an old friend about," Spadger said leadingly.

"Yes, but who—Oh, Spadger, would you?"

Spadger colored up like a bride and admitted as how she was getting a bit weak in the knees for trotting about, picking up after a dozen girls. "But still plenty young enough to look after yourself, madam."

Abbie had shot up from miss to madam in a breath. It gave her an unsettling foretaste of how her life was about to change. No more tedious hours listening to the siege of Mysore. No more tirades from Miss Slatkin for having spent too much money on art paper. No more pinching pennies to be able to afford her own pigments and canvas.

Her face looked different, when she gazed at herself in the mirror. The hairdo was more stylish, of course, but it was not that. It was the joyful smile that had replaced her customary air of worry, and most of all, the love gleaming in her eyes. She modestly allowed that her inner glow made her look almost pretty, even in her plain dark green gown. Soon she would have more elegant gowns.

Penfel was awaiting her when she took the girls downstairs.

All he said was "Charming," but his smile and the way his eyes lingered on her separate features said the rest.

Dinner was a lively meal, with Lady Penfel praising herself for her imaginary part in handling O'Leary. "Remember how I warned you gels against him the minute I clapped an eye on him? Oh, I knew that one was going to be trouble."

"Yes, shameful that he has been robbing so many innocent people," Penfel said dampingly, to remind her his other crime was officially forgotten.

Abbie was astonished to hear Lord Sylvester announced when the family party had assembled in the saloon to await the arrival of the guests. He had

184

made the ten-mile trip with his host, Mr. Sheridan. Sylvester would have been recognized as a Wycliffe even without the announcement. He had the long, pale Wycliffe face and proud demeanor. Mr. Sheridan, on the other hand, was a very dasher.

Annabelle took one look at Sylvester and felt she was better off with Mr. Singleton. Her one dance with Susan's brother confirmed it. He was an insufferable prig. What he needed was an entanglement with a female of O'Leary's ilk, to knock the starch out of him.

"What luck!" Abbie said to Algie, when he stood up with her. "I didn't know your mama had invited Lord Sylvester. Mr. Sheridan will provide a distraction for Susan."

"You underestimate me, my pet. You must not think, only because I am trivial, that I am not awake on all suits. I feared Susan would regret her jilting of me when she saw all you other ladies had snagged a beau. Sheridan is only a distraction, of course. She could never present a commoner to 'Papa, the duke' as a contender for her hand, but he will do as a flirt to replace O'Leary until we get her bounced back to Slats. He and Sheridan are staying with us for a few days."

"Very cagey, milord."

"Thank you, my pet. And now that you have accepted my offer, I can cease being cagey vis-à-vis the da Vinci cartoons. They have served their purpose."

He handed her a small brass key. "You will find them in the large cupboard behind the desk in my study. You are welcome to see them, anytime. Especially when I am there. Shall we go now?"

Her fingers trembled as she accepted the key. "I

don't know if I can take any more happiness tonight," she said in a small voice.

He led her to the study anyway, and closed the door behind them. Then he took the little brass key, unlocked the cabinet door, and drew out an aging folio. He placed it on the desk and opened the cover.

Abbie gave a gasp of appreciation. It was a sketch of the artist, done by himself in a brick-colored pastel. The eyes seemed to be reaching into her very soul.

"I shall never have the nerve to take up a sketch pad again," she said, gazing at it.

Algie's heart swelled to see the wonder in her eyes. It was the way he felt when he had first seen her. She gazed at the sketch for a long moment, then looked up at him.

"These cartoons are the real reason I came to Penfel Hall. What a long time it has taken for me to get to see them."

"Some things are worth waiting for," he said.

"Oh, yes. They are marvelous!"

"I wasn't talking about the cartoons," he said. "I was talking about"—he drew her into his arms—"this."

And "this," a very deep kiss indeed, made Abbie forget everything, even the da Vinci cartoons.